Little Secrets

No Accident

Big lies. Big trouble.

Little Secrets

#1 . . . *Playing with Fire*

#2 . . . *No Accident*

and coming soon . . .

#3 . . . *Over the Edge*

Little Secrets

No Accident

by

EMILY BLAKE

SCHOLASTIC INC.

New York • Toronto • London • Auckland • Sydney
Mexico City • New Delhi • Hong Kong • Buenos Aires

ISBN 0-439-82913-5

12 11 10 9 8 7 6 5 4 3 2   6 7 8 9 10 11/0

Printed in the U.S.A.   40

First printing, May 2006

The book type was set in Utopia
Book design by Steve Scott

For Anica, with gratitude and admiration.

Little Secrets

No Accident

Chapter 1

Alison Rose burst out of the French double doors onto the back patio of Grandmother Diamond's mansion. She had no idea whether the scream she heard was her own or came from her aunts or cousin as they raced in a pack toward the burning building. Shielding her eyes from the searing heat, Alison squinted into the blaze and willed herself to see some movement, some sign of life.

Burning rubble, thrown from the blasts, littered the lawn and fizzled in the water of the swimming pool. Alison could not tear her eyes away from the inferno that had been the Diamond pool house — the pool house she had watched her grandmother, Tamara Diamond, walk into only a moment before it was rocked by a double explosion.

Choking on the thick black smoke, Alison tried to get closer. She had a strong urge to run into the towering flames and pull Tamara out. The family matriarch was more than a force to be reckoned with and often made their lives miserable. But Alison could not imagine her life without her.

Alison flinched as her uncle Bill put a hand on her arm

to steady her and hold her back. Alison pulled away sharply, then surrendered and leaned heavily on her uncle's shoulder. It felt unexpectedly good to have somebody looking out for her.

With her uncle still supporting her, Alison watched as the entire structure became engulfed in flames. There was no way Alison could get in and out alive, let alone save Tamara. *If* her grandmother had survived the initial blasts.

The weight of what she was witnessing caused Alison's whole body to shake. She felt like an exposed nerve. Conflicting emotions crashed like violent waves within her. She was a boat unmoored.

Please let her be all right. Please let her be all right, Alison repeated her wish in her head like a silent prayer.

"Nice work."

Startled, Alison looked up to see her cousin, Kelly, smirking beside her. Until recently Kelly Reeves had been the person Alison had turned to for help in all things. Kelly had been more than just a cousin. She had been a best friend. But that was before . . . before the gorgeous, popular, and sharp-edged blond had cruelly stolen Alison's boyfriend and left her alone and friendless at her lowest moment, just after her mother had been arrested. Just after Alison had lost everything. And now here she was smiling at what could be their grandmother's funeral pyre.

"This a little trick you picked up from Zoey?" Kelly said slyly, working in a jab at the only friend Alison had left after her cousin finished with her. Zoey Ramirez was a good friend, and no pyro. But somehow Kelly'd found out that when Zoey was kicked out of her last school, she'd been accused of trying to burn it down. In less than a day the exaggerated story had spread all over Stafford Academy. Alison couldn't believe Kelly was bringing it up now. Only Kelly could joke and jab at a moment like this.

Alison didn't bother to reply. Kelly would get hers soon enough. Right now, all Alison wanted was her grandmother back.

Then, like a fiery ghost, a figure came toward them, silhouetted in the flames. Alison squinted. She could not believe her eyes. She should not have survived. And yet, here she was. Tamara Diamond.

Chapter 2

Relief washed over Alison. She ran to her grandmother, then stopped just before reaching her. Alison stared at Tamara's face, still shocked to see her alive. Aside from a few black smudges and stray hairs out of place, she looked as crisp and put together as she always did. Her short white hair was illuminated by the blaze behind her and her steely blue eyes looked hard upon her dumbfounded family.

"You're okay," Alison murmured, touching her arm. In any other family there would be hugging and jubilation. But the Diamonds were not just any family.

"Sorry to disappoint you all," Tamara said coolly, looking at her granddaughter Kelly, her daughters Phoebe and Christine, and her son-in-law Bill in turn. "It appears the contents of my will shall not be disclosed today — or anytime soon."

Alison felt her stomach churn. Grandmother Diamond always suspected the worst — that everyone in the family was after her sizable fortune and would be happy to see her dead so they could finally get their hands on the cash. The fact that it was largely true did not make it any less harsh.

"Pity," Alison's aunt Christine murmured. Flames flickered in her green eyes, making them smolder golden.

Kelly's mother, Aunt Phoebe, began to sob. "This is so awful," she moaned. "The beautiful pool house!" A wailing Phoebe collapsed in her husband's arms. Alison saw Kelly roll her eyes.

"Destroyed," Tamara completed Phoebe's thought matter-of-factly. She watched the building burn with no hint of emotion. "And all because 'somebody' forgot to turn off the gas on the stove." Grandmother Diamond looked Kelly in the eye, accusing her and daring her to deny it at the same time.

Biting her lip, Alison suppressed a smile. Things between Kelly and their grandmother had been strained for quite a while, and truth be told, that's how Alison liked it. Kelly managed to be on top everywhere . . . except at Grandmother Diamond's. She was the most popular girl at school. She could make or break anyone with a look, a word, her dazzling smile. Kelly seemed to get her way everywhere and in every situation. But not at the Diamond estate. Here, Alison had a powerful ally. Alison was Tamara's favorite — and she knew she had to keep it that way.

Approaching sirens drowned out Aunt Phoebe's wailing. Flashing lights added to the chaos, and firefighters came swarming around the back of the mansion, rolling out hoses and barking orders. Alison watched them with surprise. The Diamond estate was so large that none of the neighbors could have noticed the smoke this quickly. And it wasn't the type of neighborhood where people liked to poke their nose into other people's business — particularly Tamara Diamond's. So who had called the fire department?

Alison's question was answered when she looked at her grandmother's face. Tamara's eyes were narrow. A small smile played on her lips. She looked . . . satisfied. As if everything were going according to plan. For a brief second Alison could not believe what she was thinking — why would her grandmother blow up her own pool house? But everything about the fire and Tamara's survival was suspicious.

It did not take long for the firefighters to gain control of the blaze. The smell of wet burnt wood stuck in Alison's nose as the events of the night swirled in her mind. She coughed, and Uncle Bill pushed her toward the door. "Let's get inside," he coaxed Tamara. He had struggled free of his damp and suffering wife, foisting her off on their daughter, Kelly.

Tamara pulled away from her son-in-law, taking Alison's arm instead. "Don't rush me, Bill." She spoke softly, but the words were hard.

"Maybe you should go to the hospital and make sure you're okay," Alison's uncle suggested.

"That won't be necessary," Grandmother Diamond replied.

"At least let the paramedics look you over, Mother," Aunt Christine chimed in, acting concerned. Her performance was not convincing.

"I said I'm *fine*." Tamara spoke through clenched teeth. She would not be badgered. Leaning on Alison's arm, she stepped inside her palatial house. The servants who had gathered by the windows to watch the fire scattered. In a moment Francesca, the cook, was back with a cup of tea. She handed it to Alison rather than offering it to Tamara herself, and Alison carried it carefully over to the seat her grandmother had taken in the parlor.

As she set the porcelain cup and saucer on the small marble-topped side table, Alison realized her hands were shaking. The grandmother she had thought was dead, that she had begged to still be alive, was fine. She was sitting right in front of her, unscathed. So why wasn't Alison filled with joy?

She felt like a rubber band stretched to breaking. For as long as she could remember, she had been the rope in a fierce game of tug-of-war between her mother and her grandmother. The battle began long before Alison was born. The story Alison's mother told was that she had eschewed her mother's millions, wanting to make a name for herself on her own terms. Tamara, who did not like being dismissed, promptly wrote Helen out of her will and cut off all communication. She waited, watching to see her proud oldest daughter fail. Then, to Tamara's great dismay, Helen had made it. She single-handedly created her own domestic empire.

To the outside world, Helen Rose was picture-perfect. To her own daughter, she was too busy to care. Helen was a megastar, and a megamillionaire, when disaster struck. Just weeks before, she had been arrested and charged with embezzlement, grand larceny, and tax fraud — framed, she claimed, by her own mother. Alison had been shocked and scared when she witnessed her mother's arrest, but she'd also been secretly relieved. Helen was still in jail now, awaiting her trial. Sometimes Alison missed her. Mostly she felt guilty that she did not.

When she had heard that Grandmother Diamond was behind the arrest, Alison didn't want to believe it. But as time went on, the situation became more and more confusing. She didn't know who to believe, who to trust. Helen and Tamara — and everyone else in the Diamond family — had too many secrets to hide.

Exhausted, Alison sank onto the raw-silk-covered sofa near her grandmother. "Thank goodness the fire department arrived so quickly," she said carefully, watching her grandmother's face. "If they had come any later, the fire might have spread to the house." Tamara's expression did not change as she looked away from her granddaughter. She seemed to be studying the Fabergé egg beside her gold-rimmed saucer on the table. "I was so worried," Alison went on. Her heart pounded in her chest. "When I saw you go into the pool house . . ."

At those words Tamara's head jerked up, but her face revealed nothing. "Yes," she said plainly. She turned and looked directly at Alison. "I'm glad we have this moment alone," she said. Kelly and her father were calming Phoebe in the kitchen, and Aunt Christine had disappeared into the room she was staying in upstairs. Alison and her grandmother faced each other. For a moment neither of them spoke.

Then Grandmother Diamond set down her tea and sat up even straighter in her wingback chair. She looked at Alison gravely. "I think you should move in with me during this . . . difficult time."

Alison blinked, but only once. There was no doubt in her mind. This was not a request. It was an order.

Running it over in her head, Alison realized it was an order that might be worth her while to obey. Things at her house were not exactly peachy. Nothing was the same after her mom was taken away. The housekeeper didn't come. Her dad was a wreck. There was no food in the fridge. No chauffeur. No money. Besides, Grandmother Diamond's attentions were the best weapon Alison had in the war with her cousin. Moving in with "Her Highness"— as the granddaughters had dubbed her back when they were friends — would be worth it if only to see the look on Kelly's face when she found out. But there could be ramifications.

For the first time all evening, Alison sensed that her grandmother was tense. She did not like to be kept waiting, and Alison's delayed response was forcing her to do just that. But Alison needed time to think things through. She hadn't even stopped shaking yet. It was all happening so fast.

Tamara obviously wanted her granddaughter at the

Diamond estate for a reason. Alison suspected she had become an important piece in whatever game Tamara was playing with Alison's mother, Helen. Tamara wanted to keep a close eye on her. And after tonight Alison wanted to keep an eye on Tamara, too.

"All right," Alison agreed. "I'll move in next week."

Chapter 3

Kelly Reeves stared out the picture window in her grand-mother's kitchen as the firemen packed up their gear on the far side of the pool. All that was left of the Mediterranean-style pool house was rubble and ash. The fire outside was extinguished. The fire inside of Kelly still burned.

At the table Phoebe Reeves snuffled into a linen hand-kerchief. She was blubbering on like she was at a funeral, wringing her hands and looking as if the world were end-ing. Kelly scowled. It was just a building! It wasn't even close to as important as the other thing that had been destroyed tonight — her life! Seconds before the explo-sion, Kelly had heard the biggest shocker in all of her fifteen years (and there had been some biggies). In the middle of a nasty argument, Aunt Christine had blurted out that she — not Phoebe — was Kelly's real mother.

Looking at the blubbering ball of emotion melting at the table, it almost made sense. Kelly was much more like her glamorous movie-star aunt than like her oversensitive, overly accommodating mother. Kelly and Christine had the same drive. The same ambition. The same green eyes, blond hair, sharp tongue, and highly developed sense of self-preservation.

Aunt Christine is my mother. The idea was sinking in. But Kelly had more questions, and she needed answers. Right now.

Leaving Phoebe to her whimpering, Kelly silently left the kitchen and clicked up the huge central staircase in her Manolo mules. A moment later she burst in on Aunt Christine in one of the guest suites. Her suitcase was open on the bed and clothes were spread everywhere. It looked like a private trunk show.

"You're packing?" It was not the question Kelly had intended to ask first. She simply couldn't believe her eyes. "You're leaving? Just like that? After what you just told me?" Kelly's voice dropped to a hiss. No sense in letting everyone in on their conversation.

Christine held a strapless dress up against herself and checked out her reflection in the full-length mirror. She was clearly admiring the way the red fabric set off her eyes and her shoulder-length razor-cut hair. She did not look at Kelly. "Life goes on." She shrugged. "I have a plane to catch and a movie to shoot. Nothing has changed."

"Everything has changed!" Kelly couldn't keep her voice down now. She was shouting. How could Christine possibly think that nothing had changed?

Tossing the Nicole Miller into her suitcase, Christine turned and looked Kelly dead in the face. Their green eyes locked. The expression on her face was pure annoyance.

"Get over yourself, Kelly," Christine said coolly. "I can't just scoop you up and move you to Hollywood in an instant." She snapped her fingers before turning back to her packing, then added, "I suggest you forget we ever had that conversation."

Chapter 4

Kelly picked at a spot on her thumbnail where her mani-cure was starting to flake. The girl at the salon had told her that the "hot buttered thumb" was the latest rage in Milan and the mani would last for weeks. What a joke. It had only been two days. Now she would have to go back. But that wasn't the only thing bothering Kelly — she'd been on edge for weeks, ever since Aunt Christine left. And school was doing nothing to distract her.

Trapped in the classroom, Kelly felt like a caged tiger at the zoo . . . pacing, wishing she could sink her claws into fresh meat. She felt sick to death . . . of everything. Even her latest conquest, Chad Simon, whom she had stolen all too easily from Alison a few weeks before, was too busy try-ing to finish his history homework before the bell to pay her any attention.

Sighing loudly, Kelly sat back and crossed her long legs, pressing her calves together to make them look skinnier. She watched expressionless, as Audra Wilson, Stafford Academy's girl Einstein, walked into the room and headed straight to the first row. She was going for her usual brown-nosing seat, front and center, so she could do as much kissing-up as possible. But Audra's seat was already taken — by Stafford's resident fire-starter, Zoey Ramirez. Enjoying this unexpected bit of drama, Kelly sat up to see what would happen next. Audra tapped her foot, sneering, and waiting for Zoey to move. Zoey didn't even look up — she seemed totally oblivious.

Kelly nudged Chad so he wouldn't miss the scene. He smiled at her quickly. "Almost done," he whispered. Kelly rolled her eyes. Chad was cute and all, but he was way too worried about schoolwork. And he had no edges. Unlike Audra. Kelly had seen her in a scrap or two, and for a brainiac she could hold her own. She looked like she was ready to go off on Zoey now, but at the last second she turned away and slid into an empty desk near Chad's best friend — and Zoey's twin brother — Tom.

Disappointed, Kelly slumped back in her desk. There would be no fight. She watched Zoey wave to Alison and motion her toward a nearby seat. Alison smiled at Zoey, looked to see if Chad was watching her (he wasn't), then quickly looked away. *Good*, Kelly thought. Her cousin was still tortured over losing Chad. And she was seriously bottom-feeding with her new best friend. Socially, Zoey did not have a clue. Then again, that was why she was the only one willing to talk to Alison. Kelly had to give herself credit — her plan to make her cousin social poison had worked perfectly. Alison's life was pathetic.

Of course, Grandmother Diamond had done her part by getting Alison's mother arrested and humiliated in front

15

of all the news cameras. At least, that was Aunt Christine's theory of who was responsible. Which was exactly why it was so unbelievable that Alison was living with her! The thought of goody-goody Alison buddying up with that old hag on a daily basis made Kelly's skin crawl. Still, the Diamond estate was the lap of luxury, and if she could stop herself from being an idiot for half a second Alison could make it pay off in a big way.

Ugh. Kelly sighed again as the bell rang. The teacher was late. She was bored. Bored. Bored. Bored. Ruling Stafford Academy offered no challenges anymore. She was sick of being the big fish in such a little pond, which was why she was seriously considering going to Hollywood with Aunt Christine. She would be nothing but a guppy there, she knew. But she would be a guppy with great white potential!

"*I can't just scoop you up and move you to Hollywood in an instant!*" Aunt Christine's voice played in Kelly's head. Aunt Christine clearly wanted Kelly to move there, even though she couldn't take her that minute. She was right, of course. Kelly and her new mom would have to buy a bigger place — a place with a pool and a separate wing for Kelly. Maybe in Brentwood, or Malibu, or Bel Air. And Kelly needed to prepare for her departure, maybe even leave behind a few things for her friends and enemies to remember her by.

It still burned Kelly up that Christine had disappeared so fast. A real mother would have stuck around. This was not one of Aunt Christine's movies. This was Kelly's life! And the worst part was that Kelly had nobody she could talk to about it. She couldn't talk to her mom, Phoebe. She sure couldn't talk to Alison. Chad was not an option. And though she'd left her several messages, Aunt Christine had not returned Kelly's calls. She was probably too busy shooting. *Never mind*, Kelly thought. *She'll find time to call me back any second. She's my mother.*

Kelly was about to pull out her phone to check her messages once more before class started when someone else entered the classroom. Kelly watched through narrowed eyes as a dark-haired girl stepped confidently into the room. She was new. Kelly had spotted her before first period. The thing that caught Kelly's eye was the school uniform. The girl was wearing a plaid skirt and cardigan over a white button-down. But there were no uniforms required at Stafford — this was clearly just a fashion statement. At first Kelly thought it was lame. Who would wear a uniform when they didn't have to? But somehow the girl pulled it off.

Kelly looked her up and down. The girl's shoes were hot — tall black boots with a towering heel. Her bag looked straight out of Paris. She had latte-toned skin, big dark eyes, and a fabulous, chin-length haircut. She was pretty — if you went for the exotic type. And the moment she walked in the room, there was an audible buzz.

Kelly eyed the girl warily. Maybe she *was* worth her time after all.

Sliding easily out of her desk, Kelly walked up to the new girl casually — like she was just on her way to Zoey's desk. (As if!) "Aren't you new?" She flashed her winning smile. "I'm Kelly," she said — like the girl didn't already know.

The new girl simply stared. Her expression was hard to read, flat — almost amused.

"And you are?" Kelly prodded. By now the whole room was watching.

"X," the girl replied.

Kelly nearly choked. *X?* What kind of name was that? Kelly would have scoffed and walked away, but something told her the girl wouldn't care — and Kelly would lose the upper hand.

"Well, X, if you want to sit with us, I can ask Kate to move." Kelly gestured toward the group of desks near the back of the room that was strictly A-list territory. It was a generous offer. Most kids at Stafford would kill or die to be offered a seat there.

Not X. She looked at Kelly blankly. She let her eyes drift in the general direction of Kelly's entourage — the only indication she'd even heard what the blond girl had said — before walking away and casually slipping into a seat in the center of the room.

Kelly was struck dumb. The new girl did *not* just do that. X obviously had a lot to learn about life at Stafford. She had just gotten her first and last opportunity to be part of Kelly's crowd. Nobody said no to that — not without paying a price. But exacting the price would come later. Right now Kelly had to turn the tide. Every kid in the room was looking at the mysterious new girl. Kelly needed an attention-grabber, fast. Luckily she had just the thing.

"Guess what?" Kelly said casually as she made her way back to her seat. She leaned on Chad's desk with her back to X and flipped her hair over her shoulder. She was addressing Chad and Tom, but knew everyone could hear. "I'm moving to Hollywood!"

Chapter 5

Zoey sauntered into the kitchen, flung her messenger bag over a chair, and opened the double-door refrigerator. The thing was stocked with her dad's girlfriend's diet drinks, a half-empty bottle of champagne, a jar of mango chutney, and not much else. Didn't anybody around here eat normal food? Grabbing a bottle of smartwater, she slammed the fridge and noticed Tom for the first time.

Her twin brother was slumped in a chair at the dining room table, drowning his sorrows in a huge bowl of Cap'n Crunch.

"What's wrong?" Zoey asked before she could really think about it. She and Tom were not exactly tight. He'd barely spoken to her since she got kicked out of her fifth and final boarding school, and ever since news got around about her fire accident he wouldn't even look at her at Stafford. Zoey knew she was far from an A-lister (closer to Z) and that her best friend, Alison, was a bona fide social pariah. But she didn't care about that stuff. For real.

Apparently, away from the hallowed halls of Stafford,

Tom didn't care, either. Without looking up, he mumbled, "Just can't believe Kelly's moving to California."

Wait. Tom was depressed about the queen bee moving to Hollywood? That had been the best news Zoey had heard all day! Hollywood, with its fakey-fakeness, backstabbing, and soulless beauty, was the perfect place for two-faced Kelly. Zoey had to resist laughing. Tom really looked worked up about this.

"How could you possibly —" Zoey squinched up her face in disgust and was trying to figure out Kelly's appeal when she was interrupted by her father. He walked into the house, slamming the front door. Debbie #5 (known to the rest of the world as Deirdre — but Tom and Zoey called all their father's girlfriends Debbie — it wasn't worth keeping closer track) was on his arm. Together they waltzed into the dining room.

"Good, you're both here," District Attorney Ramirez said in a loud voice. He sounded like he was addressing the constituency he hoped to gain in the upcoming Maryland congressional election, as opposed to his own two kids. "We have an announcement."

"I'm all a-flutter," Zoey said, softly enough for only Tom to hear. In fact, she did feel a little nervous. An "announcement" from her father was never good. The last one was that he was running for Congress — a bomb that had rattled Tom quite a bit. Zoey didn't really care what their father did, as long as she didn't have to spend any more time with him. Besides, the more he had to do, the less he would hound her.

"We're getting married!" Debbie #5 squealed, giving the DA's arm a little squeeze.

Zoey felt the wind go out of her.

"Isn't that great?" Deirdre jumped up and down like a five-year-old, still clinging tightly to her fiancé. Mr. Ramirez forced a smile and tried not to look put out by the jiggliness of his bride-to-be. Always the politician.

Tom choked on his Crunch Berries. Zoey clapped him on the back harder than she meant to and Tom splattered milk across the table just as their father dropped the second bomb.

"The wedding will be in three weeks."

"What?" Zoey stared at her future stepmother, who was beaming like the cover model for *Trophy Wives Weekly*. This had to be a joke. Only problem was, her father had no sense of humor. At all.

"Why the rush?" Zoey blurted. "Are you pregnant?" It was the only reason she could think of.

"That was uncalled for, Zoey," DA Ramirez said sharply. "And I strongly suggest you watch your tongue, young lady."

Beside him, Deirdre looked befuddled, as if she hadn't understood the question. "Why, no," she said. "At least, I don't think so. . . ."

"Of course she isn't," DA Ramirez said. "But I need the pictures right away for my campaign brochure."

Zoey wished she were surprised. Her father was so calculating, it was ridiculous.

Deirdre pounced on Zoey and Tom to kiss them. "I just can't wait to be your new mommy!" she squealed.

Zoey felt like she was about to barf.

Thankfully, the doorbell rang, and Zoey was saved from having to run for the bathroom. She quickly excused herself and hurried to answer the door. Taking a quick look through the peephole, she only caught a glimpse of Alison's dark hair before throwing the door open wide. Now that she was living at her grandmother's house Alison had been coming over more than ever.

"You are *not* going to believe this," Zoey hissed, hustling Alison up to her room.

When they were both sprawled on their backs on Zoey's queen-size platform bed, Zoey spilled everything.

"Debbie #5's gonna be your stepmom?" Alison laughed so hard, she started to choke. Zoey wasn't laughing.

"Oh, I don't mean . . . I just mean, she's not exactly mom material," Alison said, trying to backpedal.

Zoey knew Alison wasn't trying to remind her of her real mother. She wasn't that mean. But just hearing the word *mom* gave Zoey that horrible kicked-in-the-chest hollow feeling. The feeling that overtook her for a year after her mother died, when Zoey was in fifth grade.

"Hey, speaking of mothers, did you tell your grandmother that Kelly's moving in with Christine?"

Alison shook her head. "Not yet. I'm kind of waiting to

see what happens. I don't think anyone but me knows that the secret is out. And I have no idea how Grandmother will react to Kelly's plan. I don't know why Aunt Christine gave Kelly to Aunt Phoebe, but I'm sure that my grandmother arranged the whole thing. Aunt Phoebe doesn't even sneeze without Grandmother's permission, and Aunt Christine is completely obsessed with inheriting her money. She's even more shallow and calculating than Kelly."

Zoey sat up on her knees. "I am *so* glad she's leaving. What are we going to do without Kelly to make our lives so . . . horrible?"

Alison's smile faded. "You know, there's a part of me that hopes she stays."

Chapter 6

Alison stared at the jail through the driving rain as the cab pulled up in front. It looked . . . dreary. No one would ever guess that the utterly tasteful and perfectly styled Helen Rose was currently residing inside. It was all so ironic.

Handing the cabdriver a twenty, Alison threw open the door and rushed up to the prison's entrance. She was supposed to be here with her father, but he hadn't returned her calls from the day before. Typical. Alison sighed. She remembered a time when her father was a comfort, protective and reliable. When Alison was little, she'd always rush to greet him when he came home from work — usually long before her mother — and he'd lift her high into the air, making her soar above the world. They'd giggle together during dinner, and share secrets when he tucked her into bed at night. But that was a long time ago. That was before the drinking started.

Alison blinked away the memories as she watched the cab drive away from the correctional facility. Since her grandmother had been keeping close tabs on everywhere Alison went, she decided to pass up the chauffeur services and come on her own. Grandmother Diamond would be none too pleased to find out from her driver that Alison was paying yet another visit to her mother in prison.

Shaking the excess water off her BCBG jacket, Alison stepped up to the front guard and showed her visiting order and school ID. She wrote her name in the register and endured a quick search. Five minutes later she was sitting across from her mother, a thick sheet of glass between them.

Helen Rose looked immaculate but weary. Her auburn hair had grown in the past weeks and was pulled back in a perfectly smooth low ponytail. Alison raised a hand to smooth her own damp hair before picking up the phone.

"You have a stain on your jacket," her mother said, pointing through the glass to a spot on Alison's sleeve.

"Right, thanks," Alison replied. *I'm fine, Mom, don't worry about me.* She felt a flash of annoyance. Her grandmother was burning down buildings, and her mother was worried about a spot the size of a dime.

"Stains can become permanent if they are not removed promptly," Helen said.

Alison stared at her mother. Was she still talking about her jacket? She couldn't bring herself to tell her she'd moved in with the enemy, so . . . "Grandmother's pool house burned down," she blurted.

Helen's blue eyes widened. "It burned down?" she echoed, as if repeating it would help it make sense.

Alison nodded. She suddenly felt deceitful for not having told her mother sooner.

Helen was quiet for a moment, digesting the information like a snake that had just swallowed a mouse whole. "She did it on purpose, of course," she said slowly. "To destroy something. Probably something that could implicate her in my case . . . prove that she framed me . . ." She trailed off, thinking. "But what?"

Annoyance overtook Alison again. Of course, she had reached the same conclusion — Grandmother Diamond must have had a good reason for setting fire to the pool house. Her Highness was as shrewd and calculating as she was rich. But it was so like her mom to make every single drama about her. It was completely irritating.

"And then she asked me to move in with her," Alison announced, wanting the news to sting. It worked, and Alison savored the flicker of emotion — was it hurt? anger?— on her mother's face before it disappeared a moment later.

Helen was silent. "You said no, of course." It was not a question.

Alison shook her head, suddenly not caring if it looked like a sopping bird's nest. "Actually, I said yes. I moved my things in last week. And I must say, it's great to have servants who actually show up."

Helen flinched, and Alison felt a moment of exhilaration. The shot had hit its mark.

Helen glared at her daughter. "Who is looking after your father?" she asked quietly.

Alison was speechless. Hello! Wasn't her father a grown-up? He was supposed to be taking care of her!

Silence. Helen looked through Alison as if she weren't there. Alison wished she wasn't.

"I know you don't love me, but I am your mother," Helen said suddenly. "And I need you now. If you don't help me, she will win and I will be in jail for the rest of my life — and much of the rest of yours." Her blue eyes locked with Alison's. Alison tried to look away but couldn't. "I know you think you might want that, but believe me, you don't. A mother makes a terrible enemy."

Alison felt the hair on the back of her neck rise. Was that a threat? Then, as the entire speech sank in, Alison felt something else. Power. She was the one with options here — her mother was behind bars! Alison savored the moment, the sweet taste of it. But there was something else — a bitter aftertaste. She felt guilty, too. The woman sitting on the other side of the glass was her *mother* — maybe not the mom she wished for, but the only one she had.

As she stared through the glass, Alison watched Helen's expression change. "Perhaps living with her is not such a terrible idea after all," she said, squaring her shoulders. "You can watch her, find out what she's hiding. Mother might be playing you, but you can play her right back. . . ."

Alison's stomach turned. She had absolutely no desire

to be her mother's detective. She wanted to scream at her mom, "I'm not some tool! I'm not an employee! I'm your daughter!" She didn't want to play anyone. She was sick of the game. What she wanted was all she had ever wanted — a normal life with a normal mother . . . something she would never have.

Alison stared evenly at her mother through the glass. "And oh yeah, Aunt Christine told Kelly that she's her real mother. Lies or truth? You just never know with this family — right, Mom?"

Alison savored the look of surprise on her mother's face. She flashed Helen a quick, fake smile. "See you, Mom." Alison hung up the phone and walked away, doing her best to ignore the pounding in her chest. If she was going to survive, it was time to start acting like a Diamond.

Chapter 7

Up in his room, Chad Simon cracked a trigonometry text-book and tried to make some headway on the night's assignment. It was useless. Downstairs in the kitchen, his parents were screaming at each other. The noise — and the effort it took to block out their words — was making his head pound.

Glancing at his watch, he saw it was not too late to call Kelly. He was head over heels for that girl, and for good reason. She was beautiful, smart, captivating . . . the perfect girlfriend for him, except for one tiny detail. He couldn't exactly talk to her about any of the stuff going on at home. If she had any idea that his family was almost broke all the time and he was at Stafford on a handout, or that he had both a delinquent older brother and an autistic younger one . . . well, that would be the end of it. Besides, all Kelly wanted to talk about these days was her big move to California — a move that was going to drastically change Chad's life, a move he preferred not to think about. The two of them hadn't had a chance to talk about how they would handle the long-distance relationship, or if Kelly even wanted to try, and Chad was not looking forward to that conversation. He knew Kelly was probably going to drop him. He preferred to live in denial.

Maybe I should call Alison, Chad thought. When they were together, she was always a good listener. He hadn't exactly told her the truth about his family — but he'd never had to pretend they were perfect, either. But that was before he had dumped her for Kelly, at a time when she was pretty vulnerable. Chad still felt guilty about that.

With a sigh, Chad looked back at his math problems. He needed to focus. He pushed PLAY on his CD player to block out the fighting. Then he closed his eyes and put his head down on his desk — just for a second. He just needed to rest for a minute, to get the throbbing in his head to stop.

Five and a half hours later, Chad heard the front door slam loudly. Sitting up, he squinted at the clock on his bedside table. Two A.M. Chad looked down at his notebook and the big drooly wet spot in the middle of the page. Gross. Not counting the partially completed drowning equations, he still had six pages of problems to get through.

As he flipped to a fresh piece of lined paper, he heard a crash downstairs, followed by a loud curse. His older brother, Dustin, was home from another big night out. Unlike Chad, Dustin seemed to have no desire to get ahead in life. After dropping out and taking — and failing — his high school equivalency exam, he had devoted himself to doomed moneymaking schemes instead of finding a steady job. Chad sometimes wished he could write him off — stop caring about the loser. But Dustin was his brother. They were in the sinking ship known as their family together.

"Keep it down!" Chad's father shouted from his bedroom. "Some of us are trying to sleep!"

Dustin stumbled up the stairs and down the hall. "Yeah, yeah," he said loudly. "And some of us are just trying to have a good time."

Chad heard the door to his parents' room open — not a good sign. Sometimes his father let Dustin's late-night entrances slide, and sometimes he didn't. Tonight was obviously a didn't.

"What do you think you're doing?" his father yelled. "It's two o'clock in the morning!"

"Relax, Dad," Dustin drawled. "You can sleep tight now. Your beloved first-born is home safe and sound."

Still behind his closed door, Chad winced. His father hated sarcasm. And if this went on much longer, Will would wake up. His younger brother already had trouble sleeping, thanks to their parents' constant fights. Chad often had to sit with him in the evenings, staying in his room until he was snoring softly.

Chad was about to get to his feet and tell them to keep it down for Will's sake when Dustin spoke again. "Sorry, Dad," he said insincerely. "I'm going to bed."

Chad listened for his father's furious response, but by some miracle that was the end of it. He breathed a sigh of relief and began to work out a problem. With a little luck he could get through the assignment and still get some sleep before morning.

Chapter 8

When Chad got to school the next day he was feeling pretty good. His trig homework was finished, his parents had been relatively civil to each other at breakfast, and Will was in a good mood.

"Hiya, handsome." Kelly wrapped her slender arms around him and gave him a squeeze. "You look great," she said. But she wasn't looking at him anymore. Chad followed her gaze across the hall. She was focused on X, who was leaning against her locker surrounded by a bunch of girls.

"Glad to see you, too," Chad said.

Kelly turned her eyes back his way, twirling a lock of blond hair between her fingers. "I'm going to miss you so much when I go to California," she said, poking her lip out in a pout. Chad almost winced. She was talking really loudly. She could see that he was standing right next to her, couldn't she? "But when you visit, Aunt Christine can get us into all the good parties and movie premieres. Won't we look great on the red carpet?"

"Sounds fun," Chad replied, brushing a lock of hair off

her face and wondering where the heck he could get the cash for airfare or red-carpet attire. He'd find a way. Kelly was worth it. And this was the first time she was talking like they would still be together after the move.

Chad closed his locker and took Kelly by the hand so they could walk to class together. As they passed X's locker, the new girl dropped one of her books in front of them.

"S'cuse." X flashed Chad a breathtaking smile. For a split second Chad forgot all about his girlfriend. X was beautiful, even in her weird school uniforms. He noticed that the uniform she wore today had a shorter skirt and brighter blazer than yesterday's version. But the tightening grip on his hand brought him right back to reality.

"Some people," Kelly hissed.

Halfway through trig, Chad realized he'd forgotten about the extra chemistry assignment his teacher had given out the day before. And since chemistry was right after lunch there was no way he could get it done in time. Besides, he wanted to spend as much time with Kelly as he could, effective immediately. His girl would be gone before he knew it. That meant he had to find Tom and do some quick copying at the break. Luckily he spotted him in the hallway right after class.

"Hey," he said, taking a few quick steps to catch up with him. "How you doin'?"

"Hangin' in," Tom replied.

Chad looked around to make sure no one was listening, then leaned in close. "Listen," he said. "Could you help me out with those extra chemistry problems? I didn't get to them last night. . . ."

Chapter 9

Tom stared at his friend in disbelief. Was Chad really asking him to cover for him again? Did he think he had nothing better to do than hand over his homework? Tom hadn't minded the first few times Chad had asked for help in a pinch — but this was getting to be ridiculous. What did Chad ever do for him?

"Sure, no problem," Tom heard himself saying. He opened his backpack and pulled out his chemistry notebook. "It's the last four pages."

"Thanks, man," Chad said, taking the notebook. "You're the greatest." He gave Tom a clap on the back and crossed the lunchroom to Kelly, who was already waiting at their table. Kelly smiled up at him, and Tom felt his face get hot. His so-called best friend had it all — a great reputation, good grades (thanks to Tom), and Kelly Reeves — the girl *Tom* had been madly crushing on since forever. And for the first time Tom was thinking Chad might not deserve it. Any of it.

From halfway across the room Tom could hear Kelly babbling on about her big move to Hollywood — mansions, parties, shopping Rodeo Drive alongside celebs.

Standing still in the middle of the lunchroom, Tom

suddenly felt like he'd had the wind knocked out of him. There was no air in there, and he had to get out.

"Keep it cool," he told himself as he walked out of the lunchroom and down the hall. It was hard not to run. He was almost to the door when his twin sister was suddenly in front of him.

"Get this," she said, blocking his path and holding up her phone. "Debbie #5 just asked me to help her pick out flowers for the big day — like we're going to bond over stargazer lilies or something." Zoey laughed, but the look of disgust on her face didn't change. "Maybe I'll suggest bouquets of weeds or poison ivy."

Tom stared down at his sister with her streaked bangs and black clothes. *She* was a weed, and he wished she wouldn't talk to him at school. He wondered when exactly she turned into such a weirdo. Before their mom died, she was normal, and great. They were tight. Now they were practically strangers. She'd barely even spoken to him since her big return from boarding school. She never even told him why she got kicked out — he'd had to hear *that* from Kelly! And yet she expected him to listen to her gripe about Debbie #5? Who was she kidding?

"Excuse me," Tom said, ignoring what she'd just told him and pushing past her. "I need some air." He shoved the metal push bar of the exit and threw his shoulder against the door. He couldn't get away from her, from everything, fast enough.

The wedding. Tom added that to his mental list of

major annoyances. It was the last thing he wanted to talk about, and Zoey was the last person he wanted to talk about it with. He was mad at her for bringing it up. Only it wasn't her fault. She was just trying to connect with him. Maybe he should let her. But talking to Alison's new best friend would not score him any points with Kelly, even if she was his twin sister.

Tom paced back and forth in the school parking lot, trying to cool down. Maybe he should tell Chad he had to get a grip on his own homework, at least for a while. Maybe he should tell Kelly how he felt about her, before she was gone and it was too late. And maybe he could come up with a way to stop his father's wedding. . . .

Shoving his hands into his jacket pocket, Tom felt a tightly folded piece of paper inside. He pulled it out and opened it. The handwriting was neat, all in block letters, and written with a purple pen. THEY DON'T KNOW YOU LIKE I DO, it read, and was signed, YOUR BIGGEST FAN. Tom crumpled up the note and tossed it into the garbage can. There was no way the note was intended for him. He did not exactly attract admirers.

As he turned around, Tom suddenly got the feeling he was being watched. Looking up, he spotted a silver Audi with tinted windows and a blue clown-head stuck on the antenna. The car was idling by the curb, as if waiting for someone. He shivered slightly, then laughed at himself as he headed back into the school building. "Right, Ramirez," he joked. "You've got a stalker."

Chapter 10

Kelly kicked off her low Taryn Rose heels and flopped back on her giant bed. She had homework to do but had decided instead to do some work on her latest masterpiece — a masterpiece to be left behind when she moved to California. It was a gift she planned to bestow on the underlings who were stuck in Silver Spring for the rest of their pathetic lives.

Kelly never really paid attention in class. Or at least not to the teachers. Lately she'd been using class time to work on her will, bequeathing her Stafford subjects with the things they so desperately needed. *Not that any one of them will ever be as great as me*, she thought as she dug through her oversize bag in search of the notebook she'd been using for her will. Still, they could use all the help they could get.

"Where is it?" Kelly grumbled aloud as she pawed through the bag. With an irritated sigh, she dumped its entire contents — makeup bag, phone, wallet, organizer, books, notebooks, iPod, and other assorted items — on the bed. Her It's Happy Bunny notebook was not among them.

I must have left it in my locker, Kelly thought, feeling annoyed. She was really in the mood to work on it. On the ride home she had come up with some really good stuff to add. She drummed her fingers on one of her textbooks. She could do homework, of course. Or she could just start over in a new notebook and make the will even better.

Kelly grabbed a small spiral notebook and a pen and scooted back to the giant pile of pillows at the head of the bed.

I, Kelly Reeves, being of clever mind and near-perfect body, bequeath to . . .

First on the list was Alison Rose, her loser cousin. Upon Kelly's departure, Alison would receive the Diamonds — all of them except Christine, who would be busy with Kelly in Hollywood, anyway.

"She may even keep the actual gems she stole from my actual mother," Kelly wrote, suddenly feeling generous. Alison would be stuck here quivering under Her Highness's wing forever, while Kelly was living the high life in L.A. Kelly smiled as she turned the page in her journal. She would *not* be bequeathing Chad to Alison. She wasn't feeling so generous as to give Alison the one thing of Kelly's she *really* wanted.

Kate Barta was the next to be reviewed. More than anything she needed a decent hairdresser. . . . Those roots just had to go. So Kelly left her Serge's services, cell number, and several bottles of Bumble and Bumble shampoo, conditioner, and surf spray. "Even that might not be enough,"

41

Kelly murmured with a sympathetic sigh. "The girl needs *help*."

"As does Ruby Sullivan," Kelly said to her empty room, tapping her pen on her lower lip. But Ruby's issues were actually more serious. Her hair was passable (barely). What she needed were some serious lessons in subtlety. Her constant kissing-up was as blatant as it was irritating. Not to mention the fact that she laughed like a donkey. She basically couldn't be taken anywhere in public — it was too embarrassing. Maybe Kelly should will her a cage.

"Speaking of embarrassing . . ." Kelly wrote down one more name in the notebook. Zoey Ramirez. She printed, "fire extinguisher" in block letters, then added two more things Zoey the pyro was in desperate need of: some taste, and a clue about how things worked. Not that it mattered, really. Zoey was a totally lost cause.

Kelly closed the notebook and flopped back on her collection of cream-colored satin and faux-fur pillows. She hoped her recipients would be grateful for her charitable donations. It was the least she could do, really. They were going to be completely lost without her.

Kelly was daydreaming about her life among the swaying palms when there was a knock on her door. A moment later her mother — well, Phoebe — stuck her head in.

"We're going to dinner at your grandmother's house tonight," Phoebe announced. "You need to be ready in an hour."

Kelly stared at her. She hadn't set foot at Her Highness's since the night the pool house blew up. She certainly wasn't about to go there now that Alison had moved in. "I can't," Kelly objected. "I have too much homework to do."

"You can do it when we get back," her mother said, fiddling with the pearl necklace she almost always wore.

"I have a huge project due tomorrow," Kelly lied. "It's for, like, half my grade and I've barely started."

"Well, maybe you should have thought of that sooner. Kelly, your grandmother has invited us for dinner and we will go." Phoebe was playing her version of hardball.

No problem. Kelly could take it and throw it right back. "I don't think so," Kelly snapped. "You and Dad can go. I'll just eat here."

Kelly's mom got a steely look in her eyes that Kelly did not see often. "We will go together — as a family," she said flatly.

Kelly laughed inwardly. What family? "I told you. I can't."

"Kelly, you can do your homework lat —"

"It's not the homework," Kelly admitted, deciding to change her angle. "Alison was really mean to me at school today, and I just can't see her."

"I'm sure you girls can work it out," Phoebe said gently. "You're such good friends. Seeing her at dinner will be the perfect opportunity to patch things up."

"I'm not going."

"Kelly, this is not your decision and I won't discuss it any further. I suggest you decide what you want to wear and get ready."

Kelly stared at her mother, her blood boiling. She was not some little kid who could be silenced and sent to the corner. She was fifteen years old!

"Mom," she objected.

"Kelly Reeves, you will do as I say."

Kelly could feel her face getting warm. "I said *no . . . Aunt Phoebe*," she said, her voice steely. There, she'd said it. She'd planned to keep this little secret to herself a bit longer, but never mind. What was out was out.

Phoebe suddenly looked as pale as her expensive pearls. She stood in the doorway, stunned. "What did you . . . ? Who . . . ? Kelly, I —"

"Don't bother explaining," Kelly said flippantly. "I know how it went. Aunt Christine needed someone to raise me and had plenty of money to pay for your services."

"It wasn't like that," Phoebe insisted, her eyes welling up with tears.

"Are you saying you weren't paid to take care of me?" Kelly asked pointedly. She could feel her heart thudding in her chest, and her palms were surprisingly damp.

"Well, no," Phoebe admitted, wiping her cheek with a monogrammed handkerchief. "But Christine wanted the best for you, and we didn't have the resources. . . ."

"So you let her pay you off," Kelly said, raising her head and daring her mother to object.

44

Phoebe's chin quivered uncontrollably as she gazed at her daughter. *She can blubber all she wants,* Kelly thought. *At least we're not talking about dinner at Grandmother's anymore.*

"I think we're finished with this conversation," Kelly said evenly. "I'd like to be alone."

Her mother sniffled and started to turn. "You know I love you," she whimpered. She held out her arms like she was hoping for a hug. Yeah, right. Kelly looked away until she heard the door click shut. The sound of her mother's sobs faded as she made her way down the hall.

Finally, Kelly thought. *Some peace and quiet.*

Rolling over, Kelly grabbed her phone and hit speed dial #1 — Christine. And lo and behold, she picked up.

"Hi, Mom," Kelly said cheerfully. She felt so much better just hearing Christine's voice. She needed to talk to someone who understood her, someone who understood what she was going through.

"Don't call me that," Aunt Christine snapped.

Kelly rolled her eyes. Touchy, touchy. "All right," Kelly said, backing off. "But I wanted to —"

"Listen, Kelly," Aunt Christine said curtly. "I'm right in the middle of something important and I can't talk. I'll call you when I get a minute."

"But —" Too late. Christine had already hung up.

Kelly snapped her phone closed, then reopened it to check her text messages. There were eleven, all from someone called "truthteller."

Kinda weird, Kelly thought as she checked the first message. She had no idea who truthteller was. Didn't really care, for that matter.

Kelly looked at the messages, one after the other. Each of them contained only one word. I. HAVE. THE. LIST. By the time she got to the fourth word, Kelly was annoyed. WANT. IT. BACK? IT. WILL. COST. YOU.

Kelly began to chuckle. This was so pathetic; it had to be some lame prank by Alison and Zoey. How stupid did they think she was?

Kelly quickly dialed Alison's cell. "Nice try, loser. Get a life," she said into the phone before hanging up. Not that she really could — Kelly wouldn't allow it. But this was a nice opportunity to point out to Alison what an utter reject she had become. Suddenly, dinner with the family didn't seem like such a bad idea. She could just picture Alison's pathetic face after she heard the message, but it might be more satisfying to see her cousin suffering in person. Besides, Kelly needed to make sure she didn't lose any more Diamond ground . . .

Chapter 11

Alison spooned up a bite of poached pear and tried not to look at Kelly across the table. She couldn't believe her cousin was moving to California — and she *really* couldn't believe she wished she wasn't. What was wrong with her? How could she be feeling anything but "good riddance" after all that Kelly had done to her? But she missed her ex-best friend already.

Playing with her gold napkin ring, Alison felt a pang. She remembered what dinners at Grandmother Diamond's were like when she and Kelly were little. The sneaking and secrets and shared smiles. They had been two peas in a gilded pod, cousins and best friends forever. Where had that Kelly — and that Alison — gone?

Alison swallowed a sip of ice water. It was the same temperature as her insides. Highly chilled. She wished she could talk to Kelly about everything that was going on. Though she had practically grown up here, actually living at Grandmother's house was so weird — more like being a prisoner than a guest. Tamara had been nothing but generous to Alison since she'd moved in, but Alison knew Her

Highness was keeping close tabs on her. She had no idea what her grandmother wanted from her. She only knew there was a reason for her being here — with Tamara Diamond, there was always an ulterior motive. But at least Tamara was keeping her schemes to herself, instead of asking Alison to do her dirty work for her — unlike Helen. While Alison knew exactly what her mother wanted, she wasn't at all sure she wanted to be a part of it. She still hadn't decided whose side she was on.

Alison blinked, reminding herself to keep a straight face. She was good at hiding her emotions, but she wasn't as skilled at navigating the family land mines. If Kelly were in her shoes, she would know exactly what to do. And she wouldn't be losing any sleep over the situation, either.

She probably hasn't given a second thought to that nasty phone message, Alison thought, watching Kelly wipe her chin with her linen napkin. She felt her cheeks flush when she remembered how excited she'd been to see Kelly's name come up on her phone. She'd actually thought she might be calling her to apologize. To talk. To get back to the way things were. *Get a life*, Kelly had said. If only it were that easy. *Give me mine back*, Alison thought.

"Alison." The sound of her cousin's voice made her jump. "How's Uncle Jack?" Kelly poked at her pear with her sterling silver dessertspoon. "Does he miss you terribly?" she added with a stab. "Or hasn't he noticed you're gone?"

"Kelly!" Uncle Bill scolded.

"What?" Kelly asked innocently. "She's been living

here, hasn't she? He must miss her . . . at least a little, right? That is, if he's sobered up enough to realize."

At the end of the table, Grandmother Diamond smiled wryly. "I'm sure he misses her," she agreed. "But this is clearly the best place for Alison under the circumstances. . . ."

. . . *That you created*, Alison thought. But was that what she really believed, or simply what her mother wanted her to?

Finally the dishes were cleared and dinner was over. Alison couldn't get out of there soon enough. Excusing herself, she hurried up to her room to watch Kelly's car pull out of the drive. The more distance between her and Kelly, the better.

Going into the bathroom, Alison twisted the gold-plated taps and began to fill the marble tub with hot water. She poured in a bunch of her favorite bubble bath and turned on the thirteen jets. As the scent of lilacs filled the air she began to feel a little better. Maybe everything would work out okay. It would be a lot harder for Kelly to torture her all the way from California. Maybe Kelly would even miss her a little and want to repair their friendship. Maybe Chad would want Alison back — if she'd take him. And maybe she wouldn't have to live at Grandmother Diamond's forever — just a couple of months at most. She could handle that, couldn't she?

Leaving the tub to fill, Alison went into her room to call her dad. She should check on him, at least. Even if he was a grown-up. Picking up the phone, Alison immediately heard familiar voices. Her grandmother's and Aunt Christine's. Alison was about to hang up, but didn't. *What would Kelly do?* she wondered. And listened.

"Don't play dumb, Mother. You know exactly what I'm talking about," Christine hissed. "The letter of agreement."

"I strongly suggest you remember not to speak to me that way, Christine." Grandmother Diamond's voice was icy. "Now calm down. This isn't one of your dramatic little pictures. I've already told you, the letter was destroyed in the fire. Did you think I burned down the pool house for entertainment?"

Alison's heart thudded. She'd been right about her grandmother setting the fire. And now she knew why . . . or at least part of it.

"But the safe was fireproof," Christine said, obviously not satisfied. "Look, my career depen —"

"It's only fireproof when it's not open. Really, Christine, do you think I'm an idiot?" Alison could hear the smugness in her grandmother's voice. She was obviously quite pleased with her little stunt.

Alison hung up the phone carefully and went back into the bathroom. The tub was so full, the bubbles rose high over the edge, creating a foamy white mountain.

Dropping her clothes over the heated towel bar, Alison sank slowly into the steaming water. She had a lot to think about.

Chapter 12

The next day Alison stepped out of her grandmother's town car and closed the door. She knew the driver, Fernando, would give her grandmother the full report on this little prison visit, but this time she didn't care. She was sick of the secrets. She wanted Tamara to know exactly where she was.

Helen Rose looked pale as she gazed at her daughter through the thick pane of glass. Alison still wasn't used to seeing her mother without makeup. She wondered if she slept at night, and what they fed her. Was her bed comfortable? She felt a twinge of guilt as she considered the queen-size bed, the ironed sheets, and the European goose-down comforter she'd been sleeping with at Tamara's.

"How are you?" Alison asked, realizing that for the first time she really wanted to know. Her mother was so stoic, so concerned with "looking good," it was nearly impossible to tell.

"I'm fine," Helen replied, straightening her shoulders and tucking a lock of hair behind an ear. "I wasn't expecting you," she added with a smile. "Thanks for coming."

The "thank-you" threw Alison and almost made her let

down her guard. She was not used to hearing her mother express gratitude. It made her want to confide in her. She resisted the urge to blurt everything she'd heard the night before on the phone. She'd come here to ask a question, to really begin to try and piece things together for *herself*. Not for anyone else. She took a breath.

"Why would Grandmother Diamond want to frame you?" she asked simply.

"It's complicated," Helen replied.

Alison wasn't going to be dismissed so easily. "Try me."

Helen Rose stared blankly at her daughter for exactly six seconds. Then she spoke. "She's trying to take away the only thing I really care about," she said.

Alison stared at her hands in her lap. She knew exactly what her mother was talking about. Her career. It was the thing that she devoted herself to — the thing that drove her to get up in the morning, to work eighty-hour weeks for years on end, to step on whoever and whatever got in her way. The thing she ignored her own husband, her own —

". . . my daughter," Helen finished.

Alison's head snapped up. She looked into her mother's face. Her wide-set blue eyes looked damp, and her lower lip trembled slightly. Alison had never seen her mother's lower lip move at all, and felt her own heart squeeze. Those words were, by far, the nicest her mother had ever said to her.

Wow, Alison thought. She suddenly believed that she could break free of the web, of those strong, sticky threads of deception and loathing that held the Diamonds all so fast.

Alison felt her fears and confusion melt away. She knew what she had to do. She knew what she wanted to do. She knew whose side she was on.

"She can't take your daughter away," Alison promised. "Because I'm not for sale."

Chapter 13

Zoey stepped into the foyer of her house and let out a scream. Through the archway in the living room she could see Debbie #5 getting pinned into a hideous white wedding gown, complete with fluffy pink feathers at the cuffs, hem, and ridiculously revealing neckline.

"What?" Deirdre exclaimed, nearly falling off the little podium she was standing on. She stared at Zoey with her doelike eyes, waiting for an explanation. "What is it?"

"Oh, nothing," Zoey said, recovering. "I thought we were being invaded by flamingos." She stared, unable to take the sight in front of her seriously. Was Deirdre really going to be seen wearing that in public? Did her father know?

Deirdre giggled, and her chest bounced up and down behind the mass of plumage. "Isn't it gorgeous?" she cooed. "I feel like a swan."

More like an ugly duckling, Zoey thought.

"Ivan, this is my fiancé's daughter, Zoey," Deirdre said to the tailor. She stared at the air for a moment, then squealed in excitement. "Ooooh, let's show Zoey *her* dress. She's going to love it!"

Zoey was horrified. Deirdre had chosen her dress for her? This couldn't be good. When Ivan unzipped the garment bag and pulled out the bright pink, puffy-sleeved bridesmaid's gown even *more* covered in feathers, she actually gagged and had to put her hands over her mouth.

"I almost think it's more beautiful than mine!" Deirdre cried, clapping her hands together like a cheerleader. In her deluded state she obviously thought Zoey was stunned with delight, not disgust.

Speechless, Zoey looked from Deirdre's beaming face to the monstrosity on the hanger. Even though the dress was pink, Zoey saw red.

"I'm not wearing . . . that," she stammered, unable to find a word for the frosted bit of fluff.

"But it's so elegant," Deirdre said, stroking the dress. "Feel the feathers — they're as soft as a kitten!"

"Excuse me." Zoey kept her voice calm despite the fact that inside she was screaming in horror. "I have to get ready for a tutoring appointment," she said, turning to leave. They would have to "discuss" the dress later. She hurried up the stairs to her room and barely resisted slamming the door. Showing respect to Deirdre was getting harder and harder as the wedding plans progressed.

Thank God for Jeremy, Zoey thought as she rummaged through her closet for something to wear. She'd never thought she'd be *happy* about going to a father-imposed tutoring session — but Jeremy could take her mind off anything, even an indescribably hideous bridesmaid dress.

Yanking a black-and-gray skirt off its hanger, Zoey slipped it on and pulled on her gray alligator boots. She was already wearing her favorite black sweater, so she was pretty much ready to go. A quick hair check was all she needed.

Shielding her eyes from the scene in the living room, Zoey headed out the door. The rain had slowed to a drizzle. She put up her umbrella and walked briskly toward the sidewalk. Hardwired, the café where she and Jeremy usually met, was not far from her house, but she didn't want to be late. The more time she had with Jeremy, the better. She was almost there when her phone rang. It was Alison.

"Hey, girl," she said when she picked up, suddenly feeling a little guilty. She hadn't yet told Alison about her crush on Jeremy, and for some reason she didn't really want to.

"Hey, can you talk?" Alison asked. She sounded serious.

Zoey checked her watch, trying not to lose her grip on her umbrella or slacken her pace. Two minutes till and Hardwired was just around the corner. "Not really. I have to meet my tutor," Zoey said. "Can I call you when I'm done?"

"Oh, sure," Alison said. Zoey could hear the disappointment in her voice but did her best to ignore it. She could see Jeremy though the steamed-up glass door of the coffee shop.

"Great. As soon as I'm done, I promise." Zoey snapped her phone closed, opened the door, and dropped her drippy umbrella in the bucket just inside. The best part of her day was about to start.

"Fancy meeting you here," Zoey said, taking a seat in the chair across from Jeremy. His eyes looked especially blue today and she had to force herself to look away and dig through her bag. She pulled out her already-finished homework assignment — an essay on Henry David Thoreau — and slid it across the table.

Jeremy's eyebrows shot up. "Is this what I was supposed to help you with today?" he asked.

"Yup," Zoey replied as he started to read. She'd finished the essay last night and she knew it was good. She was kind of into Thoreau — dropping out of society to live on your own in a cabin by a pond sounded pretty cool to her. Zoey had never been much of a scholar — Tom was the family brainiac, and their dad didn't make the same academic demands on his daughter — but she had to admit that if she let herself think about her schoolwork for half a second, it was a snap to complete. And even though she'd never been competitive about grades before, she really liked the way her test scores bugged that Audra girl. And pleased her tutor.

Jeremy turned the page and chuckled — music to Zoey's ears. She loved the way he looked at her when she'd done a good job on an assignment. He looked impressed but not surprised, like he knew she had it in her. Most people thought all she had in her was trouble.

"This is excellent work Zoey. Totally insightful . . . Your tutor must be really great," Jeremy added with a laugh.

Zoey nodded. *He's great, all right*, she thought. "He's no dummy," she said aloud.

"Got anything else for me to look at?"

Zoey shook her head. The essay was it for today — everything else had been finished during their last session.

Jeremy pushed his bangs off his forehead and leaned across the table. "You make my job easy. I almost feel guilty about charging your dad. So what should we do for the next hour?"

Get to the good stuff, Zoey thought happily. She shrugged. "Talk?" she suggested.

The dimples appeared again. "Something else you're good at." Then Jeremy's smile faded and he looked at her earnestly. "So, how is Alison?" he asked.

"Great," Zoey replied, feeling a little deflated. Alison was the one subject she would rather not talk about with Jeremy — he was always a little too interested in her and her family. Like one of those nutty, obsessed celebrity stalkers. "She's fine," she said in a bored tone.

"Good," Jeremy said. "And what about her mom? Has Alison been visiting her? I heard they're supposed to set her arraignment soon, but who knows. . . ."

Zoey tried not to glare as Jeremy trailed off. First she had been forced to look at the dress that looked like a feather boa wrestling a wad of bubble gum, and now she had to put up with Jeremy's weird obsession with the Rose family. Her day was taking a serious turn downhill.

Chapter 14

By the time Alison got home from the jail the rain had stopped, but the day was still gray.

In spite of the weather, Alison felt strangely elated as she walked into the Diamond estate. Her mother actually cared about her. For the first time in her life Alison felt sure of that. Now she just had to figure out what to do about it. And, she reminded herself, just because she was currently caught between two worlds — neither of them hers — that didn't mean she had to stay there forever. In fact, she had a feeling that an open door would present itself before too much longer.

"I'm home." Alison poked her head into the library, where her grandmother liked to spend her evenings.

Tamara was seated at a large walnut desk looking over some papers. Behind her the walls were covered floor to ceiling in bookcases filled with expensive volumes. Tamara did not smile when she saw her granddaughter. "Where have you been?" she asked, rising.

"I went to see my mother," Alison said softly. She braced herself for her grandmother's reaction. But Alison could not have anticipated what happened next. Not in a million years.

Tamara let her papers drop to the desk. She moved across the room to the leather couch and nearly fell into it. Her elegant hands covered her face, but not before Alison saw her grandmother's eyes scrunch up and her mouth turn into a grimace. Alison stared, dumbfounded, as Tamara's shoulders began to shake and an ugly sound escaped her throat.

Grandmother Diamond was crying.

Alison froze like a deer in the headlights waiting for impact. Never in her life had she seen her grandmother shed a tear. Her Highness despised shows of emotion, and until now barely seemed to have any.

"I don't want you to see me like this," Tamara choked out. "I'm sorry."

Another first — Her Highness was apologizing. Alison hurried over to the couch. Sitting beside her grandmother, she reached out a hand. "I . . ." She wasn't sure what to say.

"Of course you're worried about your mother. I am as well. Did you know that?" Grandmother Diamond took her hands away from her face and looked at Alison through watery eyes. "Honey was always my favorite of the girls," Tamara said, using Helen's given name. "I know a mother is not supposed to have favorites, but she was so spirited. So good at everything she put her hand to.

From the time she was five years old, I dreamed of running the family business with her at my side." Grandmother Diamond's voice was filled with admiration and longing. Alison was stunned. "I miss her . . . every day." A fresh round of tears flowed down Tamara's face, soaking her handkerchief.

Pulling a soft blanket from the chest by the sofa, Alison draped it over her grandmother's shoulders, overwhelmed by her sudden frailness. The old woman thanked her and went on.

"She thinks I'm horrible, I know. Do you know how awful it is to be estranged from your own daughter — to have her think so poorly of you?"

Not exactly, Alison thought. But she had a pretty good idea what it felt like from the other side.

As she spoke, Grandmother Diamond's tears dried up. But inside Alison they had a lasting impact. Her grandmother was opening up, showing emotion, apologizing. It was like she had been swapped out for her unevil twin.

Drawing a deep breath, Grandmother Diamond patted Alison's hand. "You remind me of her, you know. In so many ways. Perhaps that's why I've always had a special fondness for you, too."

Alison gulped. She grasped for the warm feeling a granddaughter *should* have at a moment like this. She was the favorite. She should be happy. Triumphant, even. But all she felt was awkward and embarrassed that even after her recent visit she was cringing inwardly at being compared to her mother. And disloyal to Tamara for having pledged to her mother that she'd help her.

Unable to find any suitable words, Alison mumbled something about homework. Three minutes later she was alone in her room. As she closed the mahogany door and heard the heavy brass lock click, she felt like screaming — she needed to do something to release the crazy feelings that were all stirred up inside her. She needed to talk to somebody about *everything*. But Zoey was still at her tutoring session. And there was no one else.

Or was there? Dialing her own phone number, Alison waited for her father to pick up. On the fourth ring her heart dropped and she waited for voice mail. He wasn't there. He was never there.

"Hello?" Her father's voice was clear and sounded amazingly sober. Alison felt instantly reassured.

"Daddy?"

"Al, it's you! I'm so glad you called. Sorry I . . . well, I'm never sure how to reach you without Tamara being around."

"It's okay." Alison pardoned him, dismissing the fact that Grandmother Diamond never answered her own phone — the help did it for her — and anyway, he could have called her cell. None of that mattered. She was just so glad to hear him sounding so solid and upbeat.

"Look, Al, we should get together," he suggested, reading her mind. "Talk about stuff. There are some things going on that you should know about."

That was putting it mildly. "Like what?"

Jack Rose's voice dropped. "I can't tell you anything over the phone, sweetie. But I'm worried about you. How about if I pick you up after school tomorrow?"

"Sounds great, Dad," she said, really looking forward to it. Maybe together the two of them could stand strong against Alison's mother and grandmother — or at least duck together under the radar. Maybe they could be a family again.

Alison felt good for a full hour and a half after she hung up with her dad. The good feeling lasted while she ate a quick dinner (her grandmother had decided to have a tray brought to her room), washed her face, brushed her teeth, and changed into the Juicy sweats she liked to wear to bed.

But once she was in bed with the lights out, the good feelings left and the rest of the day's events began to replay on the darkened screen of her closed eyes — sparring with each other for control of her emotions. She saw her mother's face, tense and fragile. Her grandmother's shoulders shaking as she sobbed. It was so strange that both of them would break down on the same day. She wanted to believe their feelings were true, but a voice inside her whispered, "Beware."

Like a stinging slap, the realization that she was still being toyed with hit her full in the face. How could she have been so naïve? Her mother and grandmother had taken the game up another notch and were yanking her emotions with their fake waterworks. And until this moment she'd been buying it!

Sitting up in bed, Alison balled her hands into fists. *Not anymore*, she told herself. *Not for a single second.* She was sick of being played. Neither her mother nor her grandmother could be trusted. If she wanted the real truth, she needed to stop waiting for them to tell it to her and figure out what it was for herself. And if that meant playing her own game, doing her own snooping, and lying, so be it.

The tug-of-war was over. Alison had chosen a side: her own.

Chapter 15

Tom stepped up onto a pedestal and held his arms out at his sides. He did not smile at his reflection in the full-length mirrors surrounding him. There were so many mirrors in the room that the place could have been a fun house — except Tom was not having any fun.

A woman who looked like she had been poured into her cream-colored suit ran a measuring tape down each of Tom's arms and around his chest, taking down numbers for his wedding tuxedo. "Is this your son?" she asked Deirdre.

Deirdre giggled and beamed at Tom. "Almost," she squeaked.

Tom clenched his teeth. *In your dreams*, he thought. His dad might need a new wife, but he did *not* need a new mother. And even if he did, Deirdre could never play that role — she was just another Debbie. He forced a smile as he stepped back down. It was taking all of the self-control he had not to make waves, to play nice and keep his dad from getting angry. Was it worth it? Tom wasn't sure.

And how did he get roped into coming with Deirdre to

the bridal boutique in the first place? Zoey had gotten out of it, as usual. Sometimes Tom wished he could operate as slyly as his sister.

With Tom's measurements out of the way, Deirdre stepped onto the little platform to try on veils. "You like this one, Tommy?" She whirled around, her face draped in pink tulle.

"Yeah, sure." Tom nodded. Something heavier — like a plastic garbage bag — might be better, but at least her face was covered. Tom picked his jacket up off the white velvet couch and put it on. He dug his hands into the pockets, thinking maybe he should wait outside. His thumb jabbed into something sharp, a point of paper. He pulled out a note. It was folded tightly, with the edges tucked in. Just like the last one.

This was not the second note he'd gotten, or even the third. Somebody had been slipping him notes almost every day since the first one. Always tightly folded. Always written in purple block letters. Always cryptic. And definitely for him. He had an admirer. And whoever she was, she knew how to keep a secret.

Unfolding the note slowly, Tom read: T — YOU'RE SO MUCH BETTER THAN THE REST. THAT'S WHY WE BELONG TOGETHER. XO, ?

Tom stared at the question mark. Not knowing who was sending him these messages was driving him nuts. And how was she getting them into his pocket without him seeing her? He only took his jacket off in class, or at lunch, and then it was usually hanging over the chair he was sitting in or locked in his locker.

Tom never knew when he was going to find a note. Sometimes, like now, he didn't even notice until after school. The notes had to be from someone he knew — someone he saw all the time.

For a brief moment Tom let himself believe the notes could be from Kelly — that she was wishing she was with him and not Chad. That she was crushing on him like he had been crushing on her for years. Crumpling the note in his fist, he tossed the thought away along with the paper. *Keep dreaming, Ramirez*, he told himself. The whole thing was probably a prank. Maybe it was Chad. Or Zoey. He hadn't been particularly nice to his sister lately. Maybe she was trying to make a fool out of him.

"Actually, Tommy lost his mommy." Debbie #5's squeaky voice interrupted Tom's thoughts and he jerked his head in her direction. Was she actually talking about his mother? "Lost," was not exactly the word he would have used to describe the way his mom was stolen from his life. And the assistant at the bridal boutique was not exactly someone he wanted to discuss the details of his mother's death with.

"He was just eleven, weren't you, Tommy?" When Tom did not respond, Deirdre went on telling the story without him while the fitter nodded sympathetically and shoved more veils onto Deirdre's head. "She died in a horrible car accident. Went right off the road and into a lake. And the DA, my fiancé, was away. It must have been so hard with your daddy out of town and everything. You and Zoey were all alone." Deirdre turned back to Tom and stuck her bottom lip out in a sympathetic "poor baby" pout.

Tom stared at her, horrified. Couldn't she see he did not want to talk about this? Couldn't she *shut up*? Not to mention she had it all wrong. His father was not away the night of his mom's accident. He was just working late. Like he always did.

The sound of Tom's cell phone provided him with an easy exit from the conversation he was *not* having. "S'cuse me," he mumbled as he headed for the door. The tiny glowing screen read "CHAD." If he weren't so grateful for a way out of Weddings 'R' Us he might not have taken the call. Like everything else in Tom's life, Chad was really bugging him lately.

"Look, man, *I* haven't even finished tomorrow's homework yet," he said, flipping the phone open. He hoped he sounded like he was joking. Or maybe he didn't care.

"No. Dude. That's not why I'm calling. It's Dustin." Chad's voice was tight. He sounded worked over.

"What about him?" Chad's older brother was always in trouble. Tom wasn't sure why the problem of the week warranted a call.

"Dad just kicked him out."

"Good for him!" Tom laughed and stepped in a puddle on the sidewalk. A worm was squirming in the water, drowning.

Tom thought Chad should be rejoicing. With Dustin gone, maybe the fighting wouldn't be so bad, and maybe Chad could get his schoolwork done. . . .

"Dustin wants me to go with him."

"What?" Tom heard him, he just couldn't think all of a sudden. The rain was starting again. And across the street he had just spotted a familiar car. The silver Audi TT with the tinted windows and clown-head antenna was sending up steam on the other side of the street. "What?" Tom asked again, staring.

A chill ran down his spine. The TT was turning up in too many places. It was giving him the creeps. School. The mall. His neighborhood. Here. He was at a bridal boutique! This was no mere coincidence. Wherever he went, there it was. Either his dad was having him followed or his admirer was not just an admirer. She was a stalker.

Chapter 16

Twelve new text messages. Kelly started to work the keypad on her phone, then threw it down on the bed in frustration. Every one of the messages was from truthteller. And this time they contained more than one word each. This time they had lots of words — her words. Somehow "tt," as Kelly had begun thinking of the anonymous texter, had gotten hold of the first draft of her "will" and was threatening to take it public.

Fuming, Kelly opened more messages. She really didn't care how many insulting things she'd said in her will or who she'd said them about. Nor did she care if people found out. That was not the point. The point was, they were supposed to read it after she was gone, when she'd already begun perfecting her Malibu tan. It was supposed to be something to remember her by. If it got around early, it would ruin the whole thing.

Hitting the REPLY button she hastily typed: QUIT TRYING TO BLACKMAIL ME AND YOU MIGHT HAVE A FUTURE.

The people in Silver Spring really did not have a clue. Glaring at herself in her enormous gilded mirror, Kelly turned sideways and her frown deepened. She was sick of this town and everyone in it.

Her mom, Phoebe, had been a bigger wet tissue than usual since Kelly dropped the real-mom bomb — making Kelly's favorite foods from when she was eight and following her around the house sniffling. Barf. Chad was turning out to be a big yawn. Alison was making her sick. She couldn't believe she was related to anyone that spineless. And that new girl, X, was just making her mad — who did she think she was? She acted like her stupid school uniforms gave her some sort of authority. It had been weeks and she was still wearing them, a different one every day. People only liked her because she didn't talk. It allowed them to imagine what she would say if she could form a complete sentence. Pathetic.

Stepping into her walk-in closet, Kelly felt impatient. This town did not deserve her. It was time to go. Now.

She pulled down her biggest suitcase set and began tossing in her favorite warm-weather clothes. Tube tops. Minis. Flip-flops.

Pausing, she grabbed the phone from the stand on her dresser and dialed Aunt Christine. Better let her new mommy in on her plan — and its new time frame.

"Hello?" Christine sounded tense.

"Hey, it's me," Kelly said casually, slipping a pair of sunglasses up on her nose. She was thinking about where she'd go in LA to buy a new pair (or three) when she realized that there was silence on the other end of the line.

"Kelly," she added, rolling her eyes. Didn't Christine check her caller ID?

"Oh. Is this important? I was just about to —"

Annoyed by her aunt's tone, Kelly interrupted. "Yes, it's important. I wouldn't call if it wasn't. I just wanted to tell you that I'm ready to go."

"Go where?" Aunt Christine sighed. "Look, I don't have time for games right now, Kelly. I'm on my way out the door."

"I'm ready to move in with you. To come to California," Kelly added. Why was Christine being so lame?

"Move in with me?" Aunt Christine laughed. "Look, whatever little mess you've gotten yourself into, Kel, I'm sure you can clean it up. Without moving to California."

"But, I'm not —" Kelly started to protest.

Aunt Christine stopped laughing. When she spoke again her voice was low and serious. "You're not getting this, are you? You are not going to live with me. Not now. Not ever. I would never have given you away if I wanted to keep you."

Now there was silence on both ends of the line. Then a click. Christine had hung up on her. Kelly stood there in her closet with her suitcase half packed, holding the cordless phone. She just stood there motionless until the phone started to make that irritating noise and the operator's voice came on. "If you'd like to make a call . . ."

With a bloodcurdling scream, Kelly hurled the phone at the wall. The voice stopped. The screaming didn't.

Squeezing her eyes shut, Kelly breathed in. It was time to pull herself together. Time for a plan B. Later, Kelly would call Aunt Christine back. She would leave a voice mail message, giggle, and say it was all a joke. And suddenly, Kelly realized it *was* a joke. Of course she wouldn't leave Chad and her friends. She was the queen of Silver Spring — capital A on the A-list of a fantastic, wealthy prep school. Why would she give that up to live with a B-list actress in Tinseltown?

Chapter 17

Alison had a blister on her heel. The new ballet flats her grandmother had bought her weren't built for this kind of hike. It had been a long walk from Stafford — a walk she had not planned on taking.

Where was he? Alison fumed. Her father had not shown up like he'd said he would. And Alison was not sure who she was angrier with — him for breaking a promise, or herself for trusting him. She should have realized that the only person in her family she could trust was herself.

Reaching the house at last, Alison hesitated on the stone walk. The driveway was filled with construction vehicles. Behind the house, construction workers were already busily rebuilding the pool house. A larger one this time, with a mosaic tile bottom and a more elaborate hot tub. Alison wondered if her grandmother was expanding it for her benefit — she knew how much Alison liked to spend time there. But since Alison was through being manipulated, she did not linger on the thought. Instead she opened the enormous front door noiselessly, slipped off her ballet flats, and stood in the grand foyer, listening.

She heard her grandmother's voice coming from the

library. Tamara was on the phone. Most of the help was done for the day, and Francesca was in the kitchen. Perfect. Her bad luck was about to turn into the opportunity Alison had been waiting for. With her shoes in her hand, she tiptoed up the central staircase and down the hall to her grandmother's bedroom.

The master suite was enormous. Though Tamara's husband was long deceased — he died before Kelly and Alison were born — Tamara still stayed in the tremendous bedroom with its two adjoining sitting rooms, two adjoining bathrooms, and dual walk-in closets. Alison wondered if the empty other half ever reminded Tamara how alone she was in the huge house, or if she even cared.

With her heart hammering in her chest, Alison breathed slowly through her mouth. She needed to stay focused. Sleuthing in the Diamond estate was not easy. Tamara was home more often than not, and Alison knew that the housekeepers, groundskeepers, cook, and driver were all eyes and ears for her. If she didn't know how much her grandmother disliked technology, she might have suspected hidden cameras and microphones. Luckily for her, that was not the Diamond style.

Alison drifted toward the sitting room with its chaise lounge and antique vanity and the walk-in closet beyond it. That's where *she* would hide anything that was important — deep in the closet. Alison stopped. She was not her grandmother. She surveyed the room again. Opposite the king-size bed was an enormous Monet painting, a blurry oil of water lilies at Giverny. Alison knew her grandmother was proud of it. She'd had her entire room redone with frescoed plaster and French silks in matching shades of pastel pink, blue, and green after she had acquired it. Which is why it struck Alison as odd that the painting was not lying flat against the wall.

Silently Alison reached out and touched the frame. The painting swung easily away from the wall on hidden hinges. And behind it was the open door of a walk-in vault! Sucking in her breath, Alison felt her pulse race faster. She could not believe her luck! Her grandmother must have left the safe open to take her call in the library (she refused to keep a phone in her bedroom), not realizing Alison would come home so soon.

If Alison's hunch was correct and Tamara had not burned all of her important documents in the fire, this was where they would be. Even though she had heard Her Highness tell Aunt Christine that whatever document Christine was worked up about had been torched in the pool house blaze, Alison suspected Her Highness was too calculating — and too smart — to have destroyed everything. She liked to hold tight to her aces.

Alison's eyes drifted past the two tall, cherry jewelry cases and several smaller leather cases. She glanced at the stacks of coin boxes and framed pieces of art leaning against the vault wall. At the back of the giant safe she saw a leather accordion file filled with papers. Without looking closely — there would be time for that later — Alison grabbed a handful of the papers and hurried out of the small airless room. Careful to leave everything as she found it, she tucked the papers inside one of the textbooks in her bag and tiptoed down the back stairs and out the service exit near the garage.

Outside, Alison leaned against the house and waited for her racing heart to slow. Now that she was out of the house and safe, she was keenly aware of the danger she had just put herself in. But nobody was coming after her. Nobody had heard a thing.

Careful to avoid Fernando, the chauffeur, Alison walked back up the same stone path at the front of the house she had walked up just a few minutes before. Then, as noisily as she could, she opened the door and stepped into the foyer.

"Hello, Grandmother! I'm home!"

Alison clicked across the marble entry and poked her head into the library. Her grandmother glared at her silently, indicating she was on the phone and did not appreciate the interruption. Turning away, Alison dashed up the stairs to her own room, grinning.

Chapter 18

Kelly hated to be disappointed. Luckily she rarely was. She got her way most of the time, and when she didn't get her way? She just made it look like she had.

It was a certainty that she was not going to Hollywood. Now the trick would be making it look like staying was an even better idea. Kelly wasn't worried. She was good at tricks.

All day at school Kelly kept her secret. She talked to Tom and Chad about the houses her aunt was looking at for them. She told Kate and Ruby and her other followers about the places she would shop when she arrived.

"I don't think I'll even bother taking most of my clothes — they'll be all wrong for the West Coast," she announced in the bathroom. She saw Ruby's eyes go big. She knew the other girls would die for her castoffs. She knew they would also die before asking Kelly for them. Smart cookies.

If nothing else, when Kelly "changed her mind" she would get some serious sympathy. Half the school was thinking about life in Hollywood and how great Kelly was going to have it.

At Stafford she was all smiles and perky excitement. Now that she was home, she ground her teeth together. She'd burned a few bridges too early — especially with her mom. Making amends was not her strong suit. She refused to apologize. But she had to do something.

What would Alison do if she were me? Kelly wondered. The thought of asking her cousin for help was laughable. But she was the family "favorite," so she must be doing something right. Kelly would take a page from her book — just this once — and play nice. It was so simple it might work.

Pasting her happy face back on, Kelly walked into her kitchen. It was something akin to walking into a Williams-Sonoma, only without the salespeople. Phoebe Reeves kept her copper gleaming and had every single culinary gadget imaginable. Though lately, not even cooking was brightening Phoebe's mood.

"Hi, Mom," Kelly greeted her easily.

Phoebe sat at the kitchen table limply looking through catalogs. When she heard the "m" word, she perked up.

Then Kelly stoked her fire. "What's for dinner?" she asked lightly.

Phoebe's cheeks grew pink. Kelly hardly ever ate anything at home. She hated family mealtime and always complained about whatever was served, pushing it around her plate until she was excused. This one little question was like a gift for Phoebe.

"Well," her mom stammered, "I have everything for a

Niçoise salad. I know you like salad. Or I could go to the store. . . ."

It was almost sad how much her mom wanted to make her happy. "Niçoise sounds great. Anything you make is good." Kelly knew she was laying it on thick. She couldn't help it. Her mom was eating it up like a stray puppy that hadn't seen a meal in weeks. The Alison Method really worked.

Phoebe opened the refrigerator and took out green beans and eggs. "Kelly . . . sweetheart . . ."

Kelly knew exactly what Phoebe was fumbling toward next. She was about to launch into a cloying explanation of how much she loved her and she really was like a daughter to her — the daughter she could never have — and she would give anything if Kelly could trust her again, and, and, and . . .

And Kelly beat her to it. She could not bring herself to apologize, but she could toss her a bone. She kissed Phoebe on the cheek. "You're a great mom," she said quietly. "Best I could have asked for."

"Oh, Kelly." Her mom bit her lip. Her eyes glistened.

If she didn't get out of the kitchen fast, Kelly was going to get hugged. "Homework," she said, holding up her bag and smiling as she backed out of the room, leaving her sappy mother to cook to her heart's content. She had a feeling there would be more than just salad to push around her plate come dinnertime.

Safe in her room, Kelly made a pretend gagging noise

and pulled out her cell. Just when she was ready to celebrate her good-girl victory she had a new problem. There was a message from "tt." Not just a threat this time, either: Instructions. Truthteller wanted money — $500 cash in a brown bag left in the trash can on the corner of First and Doyle.

Kelly rolled her eyes. As much as she hated to give in to threats, the thought of her "will" getting out now that she was staying . . . Well, it would be messy. And she hated cleaning up messes even more than kissing up or paying off threats.

Paging Tonio to bring the car around, she grabbed her wallet and hurried outside before her mom could ask questions.

With her jaw set and her mouth in a tight line, Kelly made herself a little promise. She would pay the $500 to keep tt quiet — the cash was nothing. *But,* she swore, *I'll get it back . . . with interest.*

Chapter 19

Chad's phone rang and he looked down at the screen. Dustin. Again. What could he possibly want now?

"Hey, Dustin," Chad answered, adjusting his backpack and heading up his street. He tried not to sound irritated. He wanted to be there for his older brother, he really did. But just because his brother was incapable of making a decent decision about his life, did the responsibility have to fall in Chad's lap?

"Little bro'," Dustin greeted. "How's it goin'?"

"Fine," Chad replied, waiting to hear the real reason for the call. Dustin never called just to check in. "What's up?" he added, trying to get to the point. There was no use wasting time on top of whatever else Dustin wanted. He was burning precious cell minutes. Minutes better spent on Kelly.

"Hey, good news," Dustin said. "I found a great place to live. Now I just have to come up with the rent."

Chad closed his eyes and rubbed his forehead with his free hand. His heavy winter jacket and the walk were making him feel overheated and dizzy. Or maybe Dustin was the root of his pain. "I hear working pays money," Chad joked, trying to stay calm. If Dustin thought Chad was going to pay his rent, he had another thing coming. How come Dustin didn't have a job yet? He'd had plenty of time to find one.

"I'm lookin'," Dustin said. "But I've got some other deals in the works, too. Good ones."

Chad turned up the walk to his house, shaking his head. How many times had he heard that? Hundreds, and not once had it turned out to be true.

"All right, then," he said, giving up. Dustin was not going to change. "I'll talk to you —"

"Look up," Dustin said.

"What?"

"Look up," he repeated.

Chad looked up and saw his brother sitting right in front of him, on the front stoop of his house, grinning. Chad snapped his phone shut. "What are you doing here?" he blurted.

"Is that any way to greet your favorite older brother?" Dustin replied, getting to his feet. "How about a hug, man? Ya miss me?"

Not really. Chad felt a wave of frustration as he gave Dustin a quick hug. Dealing with him on the phone was one thing. Dealing with him in person was another.

"I was hoping you'd help me talk to Mom and Dad," Dustin blurted.

"About what?" Chad's voice was flat. He wished he

84

could say no. It was a safe bet that his brother was not planning to beg for forgiveness and move back in.

"I need a little more dough, just to tide me over until something else comes through."

"You mean until you get a job?" Chad asked pointedly.

"Whatever." Dustin shrugged noncommittally.

"If you want to ask Mom and Dad for money, fine," Chad said, walking up to the door. "But leave me out of it." He unlocked the door and stepped inside, holding the door open for his brother. He could do that, at least. Dustin punched Chad lightly on the arm as he pushed past him.

Not wanting to hang around for the fight, Chad headed up the stairs to his room. The farther away he was when Dustin asked for money, the better. He hadn't even gotten to his room when the shouting started.

"You want *money*?" his father yelled. "Are you seriously asking *us* for *money*?"

"You're still my old man, aren't you?" Dustin shot back. "Or were you disowning me when you kicked me out?"

Chad didn't hear his father's response — he had lowered his voice in a surprising show of restraint. For about fifteen minutes Chad blocked out the argument, catching a word here and there and letting it bounce right off. But when the volume went back up he couldn't block it out anymore. And what he heard next made him feel sick.

"Forget it, Pops," Dustin growled. "I don't need your money, anyway. Chad and I will do just fine without your help."

What? *Chad and I?* Chad's parents must have been thinking the same thing. A dish shattered in the kitchen.

"Yeah, that's right. Your good little boy is quitting school and moving in with me."

No, he wasn't.

"Chad, get down here!" his mother shouted. But Chad wanted no part in the family battle. When he left his room a few seconds later it wasn't because of his mother's demand or Dustin's manipulations. It was because he'd realized he was not the only one trying to stay out of the fight. Somewhere in the house his little brother, Will, was probably listening to every word of this. And he would be scared.

"Will?" Chad called softly, pushing open the door to his brother's room. He looked in the closet and under the bed, two of Will's favorite hideouts. He wasn't there.

Chad checked the rest of Will's regular places. He was nowhere to be found. Chad's heart raced. Downstairs, his parents and Dustin were still going at it.

"Shut up! Just shut up!" Chad shouted, bursting into the kitchen. Dustin and his parents stood still, blinking. Chad did not yell often, and he was not finished. He glared at his brother. "I am *not* moving in with you!" He eyed his father. "If you were paying attention you might have noticed I am *not* like my brother." Then, just to keep things even, he shouted at his mom, too. "But you are all too busy yelling at one another all the time to notice anything or anyone else — let alone care!"

Everyone went silent. "I can't take this anymore," Chad said. "I'm going to find Will. Since apparently I'm the only one who's even noticed he's gone."

Chad stormed out of the kitchen, grabbed his jacket off a hook in the front hall, and headed out the door. The cold air was a welcome change from the heat of his house. He was halfway down the walk when he realized he should have brought a jacket for Will, too. But he was not going back now. With each step away from his parents and Dustin he felt a little better. But the sick feeling in the pit of his stomach would only go away when he knew Will was safe.

In his head, Chad made a list of the places Will was likely to be: a certain bench at the park, the bus stop, their regular hot-dog spot. He checked them all but saw no sign of his brother. He was trying to figure out what to do next when something caught his eye — a flash of orange near the Dumpster behind Doggie Dog.

Taking a few steps closer, Chad felt relief wash over him. He broke into a run. Will's bright orange sweatshirt was his favorite. He wore it all the time, so much so that Chad had started washing it for him while he was asleep so he wouldn't get upset if it was dirty and his mom said he couldn't wear it.

Slowing his pace as he got closer, Chad relaxed his shoulders. He had to act casual. Will was probably pretty spooked. If he caught on to Chad's anxiety it would only make the situation worse. "Hey, buddy," he greeted, squeezing in beside the Dumpster and trying not to notice the smell. "How ya doin'?" Chad slipped down the wall so he was sitting next to his brother.

Will didn't even look at him. He just kept nodding, his arms wrapped tightly around his knees. "Coming to live with *me*," he mumbled. "Chad's coming to live with me."

"That's right, Will. I *do* live with you. Chad lives with Will," he said softly, putting a hand on his brother's shoulder. If he touched him too quickly or too much, Will would pull away. His approach was slow. He didn't think he had it in him to chase Will down if he bolted. "I'm not going anywhere, buddy. I promise." As far as he was concerned, Will was the only person in his house worth staying for.

Will stopped bobbing his head and repeating himself. But he didn't look up.

Well, that's better than nothing, Chad thought. He was used to reading his brother's nonverbal cues. Eye contact was a biggie. Will only looked into the faces of people he trusted, and even then it was rare. Chad now had to figure out how to get him away from the giant Dumpster, which really reeked.

While he tried to come up with a plan, Chad stared at a half-eaten hot dog covered in ketchup and ants a few inches under the edge of the Dumpster. Nice.

"How abo —"

An expensive black SUV pulled into the Doggie Dog parking lot, stopping Chad short. The car rolled to a halt just fifteen feet away from the boys.

It can't be, Chad thought desperately. *It just can't.* But when the car door opened and the blond stepped out of the backseat, his fears were confirmed. It was Kelly.

Chad resisted the urge to run as he watched Kelly approach the small green garbage can by the bus stop, with a brown paper bag. She dropped it inside, then looked his way, stopped . . . and stared for a long moment.

Chad froze like a deer caught in Kelly's headlights. This was the worst possible way for her to see him, squatting with his freaked-out brother by a desiccated hot dog near a Dumpster. Nothing could be further from the cool image he worked to maintain at school.

"Chad?" Kelly finally said. "What are you doing here?"

"Hey, Kelly," Chad said. He struggled to his feet, trying to sound casual. He wasn't sure if his girlfriend had gotten a good look at his brother still crouched on the ground, but it wasn't like he could hide him, even if he wanted to. He would have to tell Kelly the truth — or at least part of it.

"Kelly, this is my little brother, Will," Chad said, watching her face closely. He had no idea how she would respond to this.

Kelly looked down at Will, who had unwrapped his arms from around his knees and was now making a low buzzing noise and gently knocking on his head with his fist. Strangers threw him for a loop and the buzzing and knocking were what he did to calm down. Chad didn't have to announce that Will wasn't a normal kid — it was pretty

89

plain. He held his breath and waited for Kelly to turn and walk back to her car, and out of his life.

Then, all at once, Kelly smiled, like somebody flipped a switch. She plopped down next to Will on the parking lot pavement. "Bad day?" she asked, looking sympathetic. "Me, too." She was quiet for a minute, then looked up at Chad and winked. "You know what I could really use?" she said. "An ice cream."

Will stopped buzzing and knocking. He looked up at Chad. "Ice cream?" he asked. It was a miracle. Chad grinned. It looked like the Kelly Reeves charm worked on Will as well as it did on Chad. "Ice cream. Ice cream," Will continued to repeat. Kelly had managed to use two of Will's favorite words in the English language.

"Bus nine to Baskin Robbins. Baskin Robbins on bus nine." Will started for the bus stop. Chad panicked. Kelly Reeves did not ride public transportation. But there was no way Will would get into her car without a major scene.

Kelly stood up and followed Will, waving off her car.

Relief washed over Chad like a hot shower on a cold morning.

Chapter 20

Kelly twirled a lock of hair around her index finger and smiled sweetly across the booth at Chad and his weird little brother. Kelly didn't have to ask why Chad had never mentioned Will's existence — the kid was totally gross and totally embarrassing. He never stopped talking to himself and he had arranged a napkin under his ice-cream bowl like a picnic blanket or something. Well, what could you expect from someone who rode the bus? Kelly shuddered, remembering the filthy-looking public seat she'd sat in next to Chad's surprise brother. *Gross.* But as long as nobody besides Chad and Kelly knew about Will . . . well, it didn't make Chad look any less good on Kelly's arm. And being nice to Will was clearly making Kelly look amazing.

Chad looked up from the banana split he'd ordered. "I was kind of freaked when you pulled up," he admitted. "I've never told anyone besides Tom about Will. I wasn't really sure how you'd take it." He reached across the table and squeezed her hand. "I should have realized I could trust you with anything."

Kelly felt a thrill shoot through her as she smiled back at Chad. Alison hadn't known about Will? This was just too good. Little Miss Perfect would be crushed when she found out that Chad had told Kelly secrets he'd never dreamed of sharing with her. She would have to save that revelation for just the right moment.

Suddenly Kelly's mood was soaring. Playing the perfect girlfriend was turning out to be even more successful than she'd planned — and it gave her the perfect out for her other little problem. Gazing into Chad's eyes just so, Kelly leaned toward Chad with the big news.

"Chad, I've decided not to move to California. I would miss you too much. And now that I see how much you really need me, I just can't leave." She rested her hand on his arm and gazed into his eyes. The sucker fell for it hook, line, and sinker. His eyes actually welled up with tears! Man, she was good.

Kelly's phone beeped, and she pulled it out of her bag. Flipping it open, she saw a message from truthteller. It was short and sour. THANKS . . . FOR NOW, was all it said.

Kelly pressed END and slapped the phone shut. It annoyed her that her perfect moment was interrupted. It was doubly annoying that she couldn't figure out who it really was. But she would. There was no doubt in her mind. *There is a way to squash this worm*, she thought, *and I will find it.*

Chapter 21

Zoey tossed her history book into her bag and closed her locker with a satisfying slam. The wedding train was chugging ahead full steam, no chance of derailment — and Zoey felt like she was tied to the tracks. The latest mini drama was about the cake. Debbie #5 had summoned Zoey to the parlor the night before, sounding totally desperate.

"Zoey! I'm about to kill myself over the cake. There are so many choices I just can't decide. You have to come to the tasting tomorrow. Please, please, please, please, please?"

If I say no, is it even remotely possible that she really will *kill herself?* Zoey mused. Because that was, hands down, the most appealing idea she'd heard in weeks. Well, besides the idea of evil incarnate — Kelly Reeves — moving to Hollywood. "Gee, that sounds terrific," she lied. "But I have to go to tutoring tomorrow."

And isn't the wedding planner supposed to help with all that? Zoey thought. *Dad's certainly paying enough . . .* Zoey knew her new stepmonster was just trying to bond with her over all the girly-girly stuff, ruffles and frosting and blech! Poor Deirdre was so stupid she didn't see that she was driving a huge froufrou wedge between them.

"Wish I could make it," Zoey had said, backing away from the scene. Unable to resist a little sabotage she'd added, "I hear zucchini cake is the new chocolate."

Zoey'd hoped that would be the end of it. But when the cake came up again at dinner, her dad impatiently decreed that Jeremy would come to the house for her tutoring session — that way they could study *and* eat cake. Joy. And that way the very important DA didn't have to hear any more about it.

At least Jeremy will be there, too, Zoey thought as she turned away from her locker. If he wasn't coming over she wasn't sure she would even *go* home.

"Ooof!" Somebody plowed into Zoey from the side, knocking her bag to the floor and spilling the books onto the industrial tile.

"Ooops," Audra sneered as Zoey kneeled down to pick up her stuff. "Better be more careful." Zoey glared at her through her long streaked bangs. What was her problem?

Ignoring Audra and gathering her things, Zoey got to her feet. She had no interest in tangling with the school brain. It just seemed so . . . stupid. But Audra planted herself right in front of Zoey, her gray-green eyes narrowed and her breathing a little scattered.

"I hope you don't think you can be number one in our class," she hissed. "Because the position is already filled."

Zoey stared at Audra for several seconds, saying

nothing. Afterward she wished she had laughed in her face. The truth was, she could not have cared less about class rank . . . until that minute. But one little shove was all she needed. The ante had been upped. Academic war had been declared. And Zoey had every intention of winning.

Chapter 22

When Zoey opened the door to her house a few minutes later, Deirdre was waiting for her with a forkful of cake. Before Zoey could object, she shoved it into her mouth. "Isn't this delicious!" she shrieked. "It's called Lady Baltimore. It's a wedding classic!"

Zoey chewed and swallowed the tasteless, fluffy bite. "Perfect," she said. Deirdre beamed and grabbed Zoey's hand to try to drag her into the kitchen, but Zoey shook her off. The dessert fork clattered to the floor.

"Come try the others!" Deirdre begged. "I've been eating cake for three hours and they all taste the same! If I eat any more I won't be able to fit into my dress."

"Sorry." Zoey shrugged. "I told you, I've got to study. My tutor will be here any second."

Deirdre jutted out her bottom lip. What was she, five? "But I had them deliver all that cake here," she pouted.

"I'm sure they're all delicious," Zoey added as she raced up the stairs. "Just pick one and be done with it."

Zoey was putting on some lipstick a few minutes later when the doorbell rang. Her heart skipped a beat. He was here!

Taking the stairs two at a time, Zoey breathlessly threw open the door. "Hey!" she greeted before she even saw who it was. She blinked in surprise at a pair of smiling blue eyes. "What's up?" she added casually.

"Uh, not much," Alison replied. "Can I come in?"

Zoey could tell right away that in spite of Alison's answer something was definitely up. Alison was holding a plain manila envelope and kept shifting her weight from one foot to the other. Tossing a glance over her shoulder, she shoved the envelope toward Zoey.

"I, um, can you hide this for me?" she asked nervously.

"Sure," Zoey replied with a shrug. "What is it?"

Alison lowered her voice. "It's some stuff I swiped from my grandmother." She stepped closer to Zoey. "Actually, it's —"

"Afternoon, ladies," a voice called from behind Alison. Zoey was startled. She hadn't seen Jeremy coming until he was at the porch.

"Hi, Jeremy," Zoey replied, smiling and feeling her face grow warm. But Jeremy wasn't returning her smile. His gaze was locked on Alison.

"Aren't you going to introduce us, Zoey?" he asked. He was staring at Alison as if she were some kind of super-model or something.

"Sure," Zoey replied. *Isn't this a dream come true?* she thought sarcastically. "Jeremy, Alison. Alison, Jeremy."

Jeremy held out his hand. "I've heard so much about you," he said, his blue eyes alight. He looked like a kid on

Christmas morning, and Zoey felt an intense flash of annoyance as the two shook hands. What was so special about Alison Rose?

"Really?" Alison asked, sounding genuinely surprised. "Well, it's nice to meet you." She followed Zoey into the house ahead of Jeremy. "How come you never told me that your tutor is so nice . . . or so cute?" she whispered as Zoey led them into the family room.

Zoey shrugged. Did she have to tell Alison every little thing?

"Anyone want anything?" Zoey asked. "There's about twelve different wedding cakes in the kitchen."

"I'm good," Jeremy said, sitting down on the couch next to Alison. *He* was *good*, Zoey agreed silently. Better than good. And sitting there next to her best friend, he looked . . . enraptured. That was not so good. Terrible, actually.

"Are you staying, Alison?" Jeremy suddenly asked. "Zoey and I don't have anything important to go over, right, Zoey?" He looked over, his expression questioning.

No! No! No! Zoey screamed in her head. "Well, actually, I was —" she started to say.

Just then Alison's phone rang, and Zoey was saved from having to make up something transparent and stupid. Alison glanced at her screen and instantly looked nervous. Getting to her feet, she walked to the window and flipped open the phone.

"Hello?" she said softly. Zoey could hear the harsh

buzzing voice of the person on the other end. Tamara Diamond. Alison said nothing, but Zoey could see her face growing pale. By the time she had hung up she looked like a cotton ball.

"I have to head out," she said, shooting Zoey a look and shoving the manila envelope into her hands.

Zoey felt relief, despite the panicked expression in her best friend's eyes. She would have Jeremy to herself after all.

Chapter 23

Alison's heart had begun jackhammering the moment she picked up the phone at Zoey's. "Alison, come home immediately," Grandmother Diamond had said. "There is something I need to discuss with you." Then she had abruptly hung up. Alison had felt her face go hot. Zoey and her tutor must have noticed, but Alison didn't care. She was too worried. She thought for sure her grandmother had discovered the missing documents. Tamara was far too meticulous to let something like that go unnoticed. But had she discovered something to connect the missing items to Alison? Or did she just suspect? *Thank goodness they're safe with Zoey*, she thought. *Just in time.*

As the taxi turned into the long drive, Alison willed herself to remain calm. She tried to focus on her heartbeat and breathing, slowing them down. She could not give herself away. She had seen Grandmother Diamond in a fury before, of course. But the fury had never been directed at her.

"She can't prove anything," Alison whispered to herself as she got out of the car. "Nobody saw me." *I hope,* she added silently. She replayed the afternoon in her head.

Fernando was in the garage. The cook was in the kitchen. The others had the day off. What about the gardeners, or the workers at the pool house? Had someone seen her from a distance?

Alison pushed open the door and stepped into the grand foyer. She saw immediately that the door to the library was ajar, and a light was on. Taking a deep breath, Alison walked toward it.

"Alison, darling, I'm so glad you've come," Tamara greeted, as if Alison were a guest at a dinner party. Her voice was breezy — not the same clipped tone she had used on the phone.

"It sounded urgent, Grandmother," Alison replied, trying to keep her voice steady. It appeared as though her grandmother would be going with her underused sweetness-and-light approach — lulling her into a false sense of safety. But Alison knew from experience that she could turn at any moment, and seeing her grandmother trying so hard to act friendly was almost more frightening than seeing her go for the jugular.

Tamara patted the spot next to her on the Queen Anne love seat, indicating that Alison should sit down. "It is urgent, my dear. It is," Tamara repeated with a forlorn sigh.

Alison had to bite her lip as she took a seat next to her grandmother. Tamara was trying to get Alison to trust her and let her guard down. Unfortunately for the family matriarch, it was a little late for that.

"I have reason to believe that one of the servants

has been taking things," Tamara said, watching Alison carefully.

Alison blinked. "Really?" she asked, raising her hand to her chest. If Grandmother Diamond was going to play cat and mouse, Alison was going to do her best to make sure she wasn't the mouse. She waited for a few seconds, and then asked, "What kind of things?"

"Oh, you know . . . a trinket here, some papers there," Tamara said vaguely.

Alison leaned in close to her grandmother. "Whom do you suspect?" she asked in a whisper.

Tamara looked Alison dead in the face. "I'm not sure whom to suspect," she said, her eyes narrowing slightly. "Do you have any ideas?"

Alison sat back, as if thinking. "No, I don't," she said with a small shrug. "Unless . . . well, Kelly has been here a fair amount lately. . . ."

Tamara Diamond smirked. Alison knew her grandmother wasn't buying that idea for a second, but that she appreciated a good shot at an enemy — even though Alison's enemy was also Her Highness's granddaughter.

Tamara stared out the window for a few moments, then looked back at Alison, leaving the suggestion of Kelly's guilt hanging in the air. "Yes, well, thank you for coming home so promptly. I shall see you at dinner." Her voice was clipped again. Probably choking back anger and frustration at a situation that was out of her control.

Getting to her feet slowly so as not to appear to be in a

hurry to leave, Alison smoothed her hands down her pants. "All right, Grandmother," she replied as she walked to the door.

"Oh, and Alison . . ."

Alison's heart skipped a beat as she turned back to Tamara. She was not off the hook yet. "Yes?"

"Tell Francesca I would like to eat at six instead of six-thirty."

Heaving a huge sigh of relief inwardly, Alison turned back toward the door. "I will," she promised. She hated eating early. She was never hungry.

After stopping in the kitchen to pass along the message to the cook, Alison headed up to her room. Closing the door, she flopped onto her bed. Safe — at least for now. She had gotten rid of the evidence just in time. So why was her heart still thudding like a drum?

Because you have no idea what you're doing, she told herself. It had occurred to her that she should turn the documents in to the police. From what she could gather in the few moments she dared pull them out from under her mattress and glance over them, they were very incriminating.

The file Alison had grabbed contained a slew of top secret letters, bills, and memos. It turned out that Tamara Diamond had her hands deep in her daughter's business. Several of Helen Rose's most essential employees — including her accountant — were on Tamara's payroll as well as Helen's. And Tamara probably paid them more. It was possible the documents could help her mother's case.

They also might get Tamara into some serious trouble — if Alison turned them in.

Alison sighed and rolled over on the giant bed. She stared at the beamed ceiling. Was that what she wanted? Did she want her grandmother to go to jail? Did she want her mother to get out?

What she really wanted (or at least thought she did) was the whole story. Nothing in the papers she'd grabbed mentioned Aunt Christine, or explained why Tamara had set the pool house fire for *her*. There were still so many questions unanswered — and no one to ask.

Sitting up, Alison pulled her phone out of her pocket. Maybe if she told her dad what she'd found, he could help her get to the bottom of this, or at least get the papers into the right hands. Maybe if she called her dad, he'd actually bother to answer.

It took a minute for her call to go through to her dad's cell line. The call finally connected and rang once. But before it rang again Alison hung up. Who was she kidding? She still had a Band-Aid on her heel from the last time her father had let her down.

Alison set the phone on the bedside table. No. Her dad couldn't help her with this one. There was nothing Alison could do. If she turned the docs over to the police, it would look like she was on her mother's side. If she slipped them back into the vault, it would appear she was on Tamara's side. And the truth was, she wasn't on either side.

Chapter 24

District Attorney Ramirez reached across the table and, before Tom knew what was happening, clapped him so hard on the back that Tom almost choked on his chicken. "Right, Tom?" he asked heartily.

Tom swallowed hard, feeling his unchewed bite strain against his throat, and nodded but had no idea what he was agreeing to. As usual, he was tuning out his family as much as possible. And keeping his head down. If he could stay off his father's radar, things might get a little easier. The nightmare wedding was going to happen whether he liked it or not.

Besides, he had other stuff to deal with.

He could not stop thinking about what Deirdre had said about the night his mother died. Why had his father lied to her about being out of town? It took a lot of energy to push back all the nagging questions being raised in his mind. It almost made him grateful for the distracting notes that kept appearing.

Tom's secret admirer had upped the deliveries. He was getting notes several times a day now and the notes were getting creepier. Whoever was sending them seemed to know all about him — like that he broke his arm in kindergarten and has a quarter-sized birthmark on his right shoulder, and about his Cap'n Crunch habit . . . even what time he went to bed Friday night. The note-writer was definitely watching him. The notes were also starting to show up everywhere! In his locker, his mailbox, his bag. He was racing around trying to find them all before anyone else did. Zoey could have a field day teasing him if she knew about it — if she wasn't already having a field day writing the notes just to bait him.

Tom eyed his sister across the table. Who else could it be? Kelly? Tom's pulse raced at the thought. That girl was amazing. *I'm not lucky enough to have Kelly as an admirer,* he thought soberly.

"Pay attention, Thomas!" His father brought his fist down hard on the dining table, making the serving spoons clatter in their china dishes. He glared over his plate at his son. "Is this how you are in school? No wonder you're only ranked fourth in your class."

Tom struggled not to narrow his eyes at his father. It would only make things worse.

"You'd better shape up before the wedding, son," he said. "I don't want to see any of your bad attitude in front of the cameras." He pointed a stubby but manicured finger at each of his children in turn. "I want both of you to be cheerful and smiling in each and every picture," he ordered. "And in the receiving line as well."

Tom stared at his food to avoid his father's gaze.

"We will be — because we're so happy," Zoey dead-panned from across the table.

"Watch it, young lady," her father said. He glared at his daughter. "And fix your hair before the wedding. It had better be all one color by then."

Zoey blinked innocently. "How about pink?"

DA Daddy slammed his fist down and unleashed a tirade at Zoey.

Tom let out a sigh of relief. His sister was a weirdo, but he appreciated her sarcasm — especially when it redirected their father's wrath away from him. He'd take any help he could get with that.

Pushing a chicken bone around the silver-rimmed china, Tom wondered if it was too soon to ask to be excused. He hated to interrupt the fighting, but it was still pretty early, and Tom didn't have much homework that night. Maybe he could call Chad and see if he wanted to hang out for a while. It seemed like they hadn't done that in ages. But ever since he hooked up with Kelly, Chad had been kind of lame. He only called when he needed help cheating, and he seemed totally oblivious to everything Tom did for him. If it wasn't for Tom, Chad would have been kicked out of Stafford by now. Then where would he be? Deep inside, Tom wondered if his annoyance with Chad had more to do with Kelly than homework. Both were seriously bugging him at this point.

Looking up, Tom caught Zoey's eye. The lecture was over. Uncomfortable silence had taken over. Zoey looked teed off, as usual. And totally unapproachable. He and Zoey used to talk about everything. It was like they shared one brain. But what had happened? With a cold shiver Tom put something together he never had before. He didn't lose Zoey to boarding school. He'd lost his sister the same night they both lost their mom. Mom had pulled them together. All their father seemed to do was drive them apart.

Chapter 25

Tom rolled over in bed for the hundredth time that night. Sleep was evading him. Again. Every time he started to drift off, he saw images of his mom's face — and was jolted back awake.

Sitting up, he switched on the light and grabbed his laptop from the nightstand.

"*Tommy lost his mommy,*" Deirdre's voice echoed in his head as he opened up his browser. He'd had a hard time shaking that conversation. He Googled the *Silver Spring Herald* and began to search under his mother's name, Susan Ramirez. There were several articles, since she was a prominent figure in the community — or at least the wife of one.

"*It must have been so hard with your daddy out of town and everything. You and Zoey were all alone.*" Deirdre's voice was back. Tom clicked on an article dated the day after his mom's car crash and stared.

There was a picture of a huge tow rig pulling a half-demolished vehicle out of the lake — the car his mom had died in. Tom stared at the picture. The car was not his mother's. It was his father's.

Tom's blood ran cold. He had a sudden impulse to throw his computer across the room. He did not want to see what he was seeing, to know what he had just figured out — what he had been too grief-stricken to notice five years before. His mother never drove that car. For one thing, his father never let her. For another, she couldn't drive a stick shift.

With his heart and mind racing, Tom heard an old argument in his mind. He was a little kid again. Kneeling on the stairs listening to his parents fighting like it was yesterday.

"You're never here."
"I'm trying to build a name for us."
"For us, or for yourself?"
"I'm the one busting my butt."
"I miss you!"
"Not now, Susan. I'm trying to work."
"Then when, Dante? When are you going to have time for me? For us? For the kids?"

Silence. Tom had strained to hear a word of kindness or reassurance . . . anything.

"Don't you love me?" his mother had said.
"You're pathetic when you're like this. Go to bed before you embarrass yourself."

Tom remembered tiptoeing to bed, seeing Zoey asleep in the bottom bunk and feeling grateful she had not had to hear what he had. Even so, she heard plenty. Things got worse after that. His mother was plagued by anxiety and depression. She had more and more appointments with more and more doctors. She was always taking pills and watching TV or sleeping. His father was away for longer and longer periods. Working. When he was home, he complained. He started telling her that people were talking. She wasn't keeping up with her charity work. She wore sweats to the store. She was letting herself go. She was ruining his career. And then . . .

She was gone.

Beep!

The signal on Tom's phone made him jump. He barely caught his computer before it slid to the floor. He had a text message.

Chapter 26

"No, listen to this." Zoey dumped her popcorn tub in the trash, stopped in the middle walkway of the movie theater, and held up both hands, palms facing Alison. She needed her friend's full attention for this one. She spoke slowly. "They are actually going to have an ice sculpture carved in Deirdre's likeness. An ice sculpture!"

Alison choked on her Diet Coke. She covered her mouth so she wouldn't spray anyone and threw the drink away. The Ramirez wedding was going to be something else.

"I can't believe I'm going to be legally related to her." Zoey pushed open the door and they exited the theater into the slanted light of late afternoon. They had decided to hit a matinee since they were both feeling a serious need to escape their houses. The movie was lame, but it felt good to vent to someone who got it. "I'm glad you'll be there to witness the spectacle in person — before it's in all the papers. I mean, not that I want *anyone* to see me in that dress. . . . Did I tell you that Tom has to wear a pink tie and cummerbund?"

Alison cringed. "That is so eighties," she groaned.

"And he isn't even complaining." It was beyond Zoey

how her brother could take all of this insanity in stride. He wasn't whining or getting mad or . . . come to think of it, he wasn't doing anything. He wasn't saying a word. He was practically a zombie — a far cry from the brother she used to know. "Maybe he was brainwashed when I was away at school." Zoey smirked at the idea. If it would make him a better son-of-a-candidate, her dad might actually do it.

"Maybe he's just distracted," Alison suggested, leading them toward a café. "He works pretty hard at school and stuff. And he doesn't have a tutor like you." Alison nudged Zoey playfully.

Zoey bristled. Why was Alison bringing up Jeremy? Her best friend and her tutor seemed waaay too interested in each other.

"He's cute, huh?" she said casually, searching Alison's face for a reaction. She really hoped Alison didn't have a crush on him. She wasn't sure she could take that.

"Definitely. I don't know how you get any studying done," Alison teased. "It must be hard to concentrate."

Zoey's heart dropped as she got in line. "So do you like him?" she asked. She didn't want to hear it, but she had to know.

"No! I mean, yes. But not like that! For you. You know."

Zoey felt the hairs on the back of her neck lay back down while Alison stammered on, tripping over her own tongue. She believed Alison was not interested in Jeremy. If she was, she wouldn't have teased. Her sense of humor was not that biting. Come to think of it, Alison's humor was a lot like Jeremy's. Both of them were fun and liked to joke around, but not in a mean way.

Knowing Alison wasn't into Jeremy only solved half of Zoey's problem, though. Jeremy was definitely obsessed with the Rose family. And if Jeremy — nice, safe, sweet Jeremy — decided to go after Alison, how could Zoey object? Because, let's face it, the girl didn't get a lot of "nice" in her life.

"Whatever." Zoey shrugged the whole thing off, changing the subject. "At least I'm doing well in school."

"Um. That's an understatement."

"Yeah, well, it seems to have earned me a new best enemy," Zoey said.

"Who, Audra? Don't worry about her — she's always been like that," Alison said.

"Like what? Crazy?"

With their drinks in hand, the girls found a table by a window so they could watch the shoppers go by. They sat silently for a minute, then Zoey leaned across the small table. "So, are you gonna tell me what's in those papers you needed me to stash the other night?"

Alison leaned in, too, lowering her voice until it was almost a whisper. "They have to do with the key to the case against my mom," she said. "It's totally crazy. I know I can trust you. But I don't know what to do, Zoey. My grandmother is involved in the whole thing. She's the reason my mom is in jail and now I'm *living* with her. If she found out I have evidence against her can you imagine what she'd do to *me*? What if I showed someone the papers and my mom still got convicted? I mean, just because my grandmother is involved, that doesn't mean my mom is innocent."

Alison looked completely spooked. For a second Zoey was sorry she'd brought it up. She'd wanted Alison to tell her about the papers so she wouldn't feel so guilty about having looked at them. She'd figured out that some of them were accounting papers, payroll or something, but the names on them had not been familiar at all . . . except for Tamara's. She'd had no idea they were a key piece of evidence in the biggest trial in the state. DA Daddy would probably kill to get his hands on them. Good thing he wasn't Helen Rose's prosecutor.

"Should I give them to my mom's lawyers?" Alison's blue eyes were pleading. She was shouldering a heavy burden and looking to unload.

Zoey wished she could help. But she didn't really trust lawyers — especially her own father. "I wish I could tell you what to do," Zoey said. "But to tell you the truth, I have absolutely no idea."

Chapter 27

The door to the chemistry lab opened and students filed out. Chad pushed his way in, like a salmon swimming upstream. Quickly he made his way over to the table where he and Kelly always sat. Chad had been surprised when Kelly'd offered to pair up with him at the beginning of the school year — Chad was still with Alison back then. He probably would be getting a better grade now if he'd said no and signed up with Tom, but he had the hottest partner on campus — and that had to count for something. Smiling to himself, Chad fished his work out of his bag.

Ever since the big blowup at his house, he had been feeling better. His parents were fighting less, which was helping Will settle down and sleep better. Dustin hadn't called in almost a week. And the best yet — Kelly was not moving away. It seemed like his luck was on an upswing. He hadn't felt this good since . . . well, since he and Alison first got together. Now that he thought about it, it felt a lot like that. Maybe it was because he knew he could really trust Kelly now. That she was always going to be there for him. She was so nice to Will, he felt bad for ever thinking she would have a problem with him.

Really, Kelly's response to his little brother was more than Chad could have hoped for. He was falling for Kelly in a whole new way. Maybe soon he would tell her about the other things going on with him, like his family, his money troubles, and his free ride at school. Maybe she wouldn't care. She liked *him*, right? That other stuff didn't matter.

Chad popped open a Red Bull and settled in to finish his homework before the bell. He had skipped breakfast, as usual. He never had an appetite in the morning. But when he was getting dressed he noticed he had to tighten his belt another notch. He was so busy lately that he was losing weight. His clothes had gotten a little baggy.

Sliding onto the stool beside him, Kelly flashed Chad her electric smile. "You know, there's a reason they call it *home*work," she joked. "You're supposed to do it at home."

"I know." Chad smiled back, turning his full attention to Kelly. He loved the way she sat on the stool, hooking the heel of one boot on the cross bar and slinging one leg over the other. "I got kinda busy with Will and . . ." Chad trailed off when he saw Kelly looking at that new girl, X, on the other side of the room. He didn't want to bore Kelly with details of his home life. "Almost done," he apologized.

Tom came in and sat down with Audra, his lab partner, without looking their way. Chad tried to catch his eye, to let him know he was doing his own work today, but Tom never looked over.

Mr. Thomsen collected the papers as soon as the bell

rang. Chad had finished all but one. Not bad. Now if he could just stay awake through class . . .

Chad's eyes crossed and his head lolled dangerously on his shoulders when a buzzing in his jacket pocket startled him awake. His cell phone was vibrating. Who in the world would call him during class? Getting to his feet, he lunged across the room for the bathroom pass and made it out to the corridor before the phone rang a third time.

"Hello?" He held his breath as he hurried down the hall, hoping the call had nothing to do with Will.

"Bro'."

Dustin. Why hadn't he looked at the caller ID?

"Oh, it's you." Chad was hardly ever happy to hear from Dustin. Today was no different. "What do you want?" he asked, sitting down on the stairs.

"Why you gotta be like that?" Dustin sounded hurt. "Why do you always think the worst?"

"You called me during chemistry."

"Right. You're in school. Right. I'll get to the point. I just called to say bye."

"Good-bye?"

"Right. I'm taking off for a little while. Pursuing a business interest out of town. But I need you to cover for me. Tell Mom and Dad you've seen me around at my new place, okay?"

Chad groaned. Whatever Dustin was up to, Chad didn't

want to be involved. "So you're *not* moving into the new place?"

"No, and —"

"So, where have you been living?" Chad pictured Dustin on the streets, sleeping under cardboard like the people in doorways in D.C.

"Don't worry, everything's cool. I'll catch you later. Thanks for everything, little bro'."

"Hey. Where are you?" Chad asked again. But there was no response. The line was dead.

A sharp pain under his brow forced Chad to close his eyes tightly. A warm trickle of blood on his face made them fly open again. He had a bloody nose — a gusher — and nothing to stop the flow with. Leaning over so he would not get blood on his shirt, he watched it drip in dark red circles on the tile. Carefully he pinched his nostrils closed and tipped his head back. He couldn't see much, but if he could just get to the bathroom . . .

"Need a hand?"

The voice was familiar. Cocking his head a little, Chad could just see Alison on the landing above him. They hadn't talked since that night in Tamara Diamond's pool. Chad hadn't thought they would ever talk again and felt suddenly guilty at how happy he was to hear her voice.

"Oh, Chad!" Alison hurried down the steps, digging in her purse for some tissues. She pressed them into Chad's hand, the one holding his nose, and took him by the other

119

elbow. "Whoa." She looked at the floor. "That's a lot of blood. Did somebody punch you?"

"No," Chad said through his pinched and muffled nose, though in a weird way he did feel like he had just suffered a major blow.

Chapter 28

Leading Chad through the halls of Stafford, Alison felt like she was having déjà vu. Being close to her ex felt so familiar. Except for the fact that he had blood gushing out of his nose, it was like old times.

Alison suddenly felt a little self-conscious — and bitter. "Where's Kelly when you need her? California?" she said lightly. Bringing up Kelly caused a sour taste in her mouth, but Alison didn't want Chad to think she'd forgotten he was taken. Just because she was helping him didn't mean she was hoping they'd get back together.

"Didn't you hear? She's not going." Chad's voice was muffled in a wad of tissue.

Alison stopped in front of the nurse's door and let that sink in. Kelly was not moving. Her best-friend-turned-worst-enemy was staying in Silver Spring, where she could continue destroying Alison's life, just for the fun of it. As a sense of unease spread from Alison's gut, she felt something else — a little glimmer of hope.

Ugh. Alison shook off the news, pulled open the door to the nurse's office, and practically shoved Chad inside. "Here you go," she said lightly. Then, before Chad could even say thank you, Alison took off. She raced down the hall and into the girls' room. It was empty. Leaning over the sink, Alison splashed cold water on her cheeks, trying to wash away her lame hopes of reviving the past. That life she had — the one she used to share with Kelly and Chad and even her mother — was over. And after what they had done to her — all of them — she should have been glad.

It was pathetic to wish she had them all back again. And pathetic was the last thing Alison wanted to be. "Get over it," she told her reflection in the mirror.

Pushing Chad and Kelly and her mother out of her mind, Alison shoved open the bathroom's swinging door and stepped into the hall. She was startled to see X standing there, and blushed. Had X heard anything? It was hard not to feel pathetic when people caught you talking to yourself in bathrooms.

"Hey." Alison tried to pretend she wasn't dying of embarrassment.

X looked at her like she had just noticed her — even though Alison had almost clocked her with the door a second earlier.

"Oh, hey. Alison, right?"

"Yeah." Alison was surprised that X knew who she was. Most of the nasty rumors Kelly had started about Alison right after ditching her had died down by now. X, on the other hand, was the name on the tip of everybody's tongue — and after only being at school a couple of weeks.

She probably saw me in the tabloids, Alison thought wryly. Her mother's rep was enough for both of them right now.

As X walked past her into the bathroom, Alison caught herself grinning stupidly. She was flattered X knew her, regardless of why. The new girl was undeniably cool. She was like a cat, the way she silently slipped in unannounced — and was always so aloof. She didn't seem to care who liked her and who didn't. Which just made everybody interested.

Alison felt a shiver of envy. It would be such a relief if she just didn't care what people thought.

Chapter 29

Tom opened the front door to his house and made a beeline to his room. He had no idea if Deirdre was even home, but he wasn't taking any chances. If he had to listen to one more nauseating wedding detail he would seriously lose it.

Besides, he needed some time to think. Ever since he'd discovered the online photo of his mother's death scene he'd been a little freaked. Because there was really only one way his dad's car could have been there: if his dad was there. And if his dad was there . . .

Tom threw himself onto his bed and stared out the window at the red and gold leaves on the trees outside. Fall was his mother's favorite time of year, and his, too — at least until she died in it.

Tom closed his eyes and tried to remember what he could about the night his mother died. Zoey had been with Alison at a slumber party at Kelly's house, their dad had been working late as usual, and he and his mom were having dinner alone. He remembered her being on the phone with his dad, arguing. She asked him to come home so they could talk, and he refused.

Tom remembered thinking that he was going to make

her laugh during dinner, make her happy. She'd seemed so sad lately.

But that night was worse, if anything. She broke down right at the table, sobbing.

"Mom, what's wrong?" Tom had asked, cuddling up to her. He desperately wanted to make his mom feel better but had no idea how — he was only a fifth grader, and his mom was clinically depressed.

His mother wiped her face on her napkin. "Nothing, sweetie," she'd replied, smiling weakly through her tears. But a few minutes later she pushed her chair back and kissed him on the head. "I'm not feeling very well," she'd said. "I'm going to bed."

Tom felt his chest ache at the memory of watching his mother leave the dining room, her shoulders slumped with sadness.

He'd stayed up past his bedtime watching TV, waiting for his dad to come home, but he fell asleep on the couch before that happened. When he woke up, he discovered that he was alone in the house.

"Mom?" he'd called, rushing from room to room. There was an empty bottle of prescription pills on the counter by the bathroom sink. A few of the pills had fallen to the floor. But his mother was not there.

Tom sat up in bed a little, his heart pounding as he remembered how scared he'd been when he'd realized his mom wasn't home.

Tom had grabbed the phone and called his dad's office,

but nobody picked up. Zoey got the next call, at Kelly's. Tom didn't have to say much, just mention their mom's name. Zoey was home in half an hour. The two of them huddled on the sofa for what felt like hours, waiting. . . .

Finally, around midnight, their father came home and told them that there'd been a terrible accident.

A loud sob escaped Tom's throat. He jumped to his feet and tried to shut out the memory of that moment, that second when his entire life changed forever.

"Your mother is dead."

Tom pulled out the photo he'd printed from his computer and stared at his father's half-submerged car — the car his mother died in.

He remembered the way his father had broken the news, as if he were reporting that they had run out of milk. He was so detached, so distant as he told them that she had driven her car into a lake.

Tom had never questioned that — until he saw this photo. Since then, he'd been full of questions.

And deep in his gut, he knew there was only one answer.

Chapter 30

No matter how many times she visited, the Silver Spring jail always gave Alison the creeps. It was even scarier when she had to tell her mother something Helen didn't want to hear.

"I looked everywhere," Alison lied. "I didn't find anything."

"Everywhere? Even in Mother's bedroom?" Helen Rose stared evenly at her daughter's face. Even through thick glass, her stare was intimidating.

"Everywhere." Alison tried to hold her mother's gaze but had to look away. She reminded herself that her mother was locked up — there was nothing Helen could do to get back at her.

There was a long moment of silence. And then, "You'll just have to look harder," Helen said flatly. "I'm counting on you to do this, Alison. It's our only hope of surviving."

You mean your *only hope,* Alison said in her head. But she nodded.

"Well," Helen said sharply, "I guess you must have schoolwork or something."

"Yeah. I better go." Alison hung up the phone and

ducked out. Her mother's dismissive tone would have irked her if she weren't so relieved to go.

Seated comfortably in the back of a taxi, Alison flipped open her phone. She still hadn't reached her dad, let alone seen him, since he stood her up over a week ago. He had only left one message since then, and he hadn't exactly sounded sober. Alison hit SEND and held her breath.

After the fourth ring, his voice mail picked up. "You've reached Jack Rose. Leave a message and I'll return your call."

Yeah, right. "Hey, Dad. This is Alison. You know, your daughter," she added wryly. "Maybe you could call me sometime. Let me know if you're still alive."

As she was hanging up the phone, it rang.

"Sweetheart, it's Dad."

"Dad?" He sounded out of breath. "Where are you?"

"Sorry I've been hard to reach. You're okay, right?"

"Um, yeah. I guess so." Why was her dad being so weird?

"Good. Look — I know things are hard right now, but I just need you to be really . . . careful. Can you promise me that?"

Careful? "Daddy, what's going on?" Alison was getting annoyed — and worried. Was her dad just drunk, or was he trying to tell her something?

"Sorry, I can't talk right now," he blurted. "I'll call you soon. Just . . . take good care of yourself."

"Dad?"

But her dad didn't answer. He'd already hung up.

Chapter 31

The news that Kelly had chosen to stay in Silver Spring spread fast — just like she knew it would. Soon everyone was rejoicing, including her mom. It was like some sort of homecoming — except she never left. For a few days, Kelly sat back and soaked it up.

She strutted the halls of Stafford with her devoted golden boy on her arm. She once again ruled the school. X was all but forgotten.

Capitalizing on her reign, Kelly made sure to walk past Alison several times a day so she could not miss Chad's fresh attentiveness. The boy hardly glanced away from her — like she was a dream he did not want to wake up from. Given what she'd learned about his family, she could hardly blame him. There was no doubt she was the best thing in his life. Ever.

And Tom had been as happy as Chad to find out she was staying. Maybe even happier. *He's probably in love with me, too,* Kelly thought. She let that thought play in her head a while. *Now that could be interesting.*

By midweek Kelly had grown bored with the welcome-back party. All of the celebrating and sweetness was starting to make her sick. And something else was bothering her, too. Her view from the top was only shadowed by one thing — her position at her grandmother's house. Kelly was losing that turf battle with Alison.

A frown marred Kelly's pretty face. She hated to think Alison had anything to lord over her — and Her Highness was a powerful ace. Suddenly Kelly wanted her grandmother's respect. She wanted Tamara to see that Kelly was strong, and ruthless, and a worthwhile ally. That she, not Alison, had learned Her Highness's lessons well.

Kelly threw back her shoulders as a slow smile appeared on her face. She had work to do, but did not doubt she could make up lost ground and capture more. Two thoughts strengthened her resolve: Kelly deserved to have Grandmother Diamond on *her* side. And when she did, Alison would have no one.

Chapter 32

Alison sat next to her grandmother in the second row of the vaulted cathedral. They weren't family of the bride or the groom, but being the richest woman in town had its perks.

As does being her favorite granddaughter, Alison thought, fingering the diamond pendant she wore around her neck. Tamara had purchased it for her just for the wedding, along with a new dress and Jimmy Choo slingbacks. She looked great.

Alison glanced around the inside of the cathedral. Even though Zoey had warned her what to expect, it was still pretty overwhelming. The entire cathedral was decked out in pale pink. Pink flowers, pink banners, pink ribbons, pink candles . . . even a pink carpet up the aisle. The flowers alone — towering bouquets of roses and lilies and freesia and orchids — must have cost a fortune. The whole thing had a nauseating effect and made Alison wish for one more pink thing — a bottle of Pepto-Bismol.

Silver Spring's see-and-be-seen elite were there in force, dressed to the nines and gossiping discreetly while they waited for the ceremony to begin. Alison recognized most of them from her grandmother's soirees, her mother's formal dinner parties, and the stuffy, extravagant charity fund-raisers that had been so much more bearable to attend back when she was friends with Kelly.

Suddenly the doors at the back of the cathedral swung open, and the twelve-piece orchestra in the pink-draped balcony began to play the wedding march. Alison craned her neck for a glimpse of Zoey, but couldn't get a line of sight over the hundreds of heads all turned to look at the wedding party. But the suspense didn't last long. Decked out in black tails with a white silk tie and large diamond cufflinks — DA Ramirez looked smug as he strode up to the altar to stand before the minister. Then, from the side of the cathedral, several groomsmen approached to stand next to the groom. Tom looked ultragrumpy and stiff in his tuxedo, but Alison couldn't help noticing how adorable he looked, too. The pink tie brought out the color in his cheeks and was a nice contrast to his dark eyes.

Turning her attention back to the rear of the cathedral, Alison almost laughed out loud when she saw Zoey in the doorway. The flamingo dress really was as bad as she'd said. Blatantly forcing a smile, Alison's best friend made her way up the aisle in the pinkest, featheriest, poofiest dress Alison had ever seen. At least she looked better in it than Deirdre's other bridesmaids, who followed behind.

Alison tried to smile reassuringly as Zoey passed her row. Zoey mouthed the words "help me," then quickly checked to make sure her father wasn't looking. He was too busy nodding at the reporters seated in the front row "family" seats and displaying his strong profile for the photographers. Alison had to admit she was glad it was Zoey and not her taking part in this circus. She'd had enough humiliation lately.

Finally it was Deirdre's turn to walk down the aisle. She waltzed along the pink carpet, giving the audience little waves with her free hand and giggling as she got closer to her groom. She seemed completely oblivious to the fact that she looked more like a Vegas showgirl than a bride.

I can't believe she'll be Zoey's stepmother, Alison thought as she passed. Two more different females did not exist on the planet.

"Oh, Dante," Alison heard her grandmother murmur. "What are you marrying?"

Alison hid a smile, then eyed the elderly woman standing absurdly erect next to her with a bit of suspicion. Why would Tamara Diamond even remotely care who DA Ramirez married?

When the ceremony was finally over, the orchestra played a rousing march and everyone threw pink rose petals on the bride and groom as they walked arm in arm back down the aisle. Deirdre looked like she was about to burst with excitement. There was no question: As a little girl she'd played "bride" with a vengance.

"Find me as soon as you can at the reception," Zoey murmured as she walked by awkwardly. Her heels and the thick pink carpet were obviously a treacherous combination.

"I will," Alison promised. She took her grandmother by the arm and began to lead her out of the cathedral. But their progress was impeded by a guest hoping to pay homage to Her Royal Highness, Tamara Diamond.

"What a lovely dress, Mrs. Diamond," the woman cooed, nearly stepping on Alison's toes. "Wherever did you find it?"

Tamara looked at her admirer as if she were a speck of dirt on her favorite Oriental rug. "At a clothing store, of course," she said witheringly.

Alison bit her tongue. Her grandmother could be so rude!

Without another word to anybody, Tamara led Alison out of the cathedral and into their waiting car.

"The public! Good grief!" she complained as she closed the door.

"But they adore you. She was just trying to be nice, Grandmother," Alison said softly.

"Nobody is nice for no reason," Tamara replied flatly. "Remember that, Alison."

Alison said nothing as the car pulled away from the curb and made the short drive to the country club.

"Stay close," Tamara instructed as the car came to a halt. "I don't want to be left alone."

So much for having a good time, Alison thought as they made their way into the clubhouse. But as soon as she

134

stepped inside she forgot about her grandmother's mood. If the church was lavishly decorated, the country club was a riot. Pink was everywhere, of course — even in the champagne fountains. The ice sculpture of the bride seemed to have been nixed, but there were flamingoes carved from pink ice standing on pink-draped pedestals.

Servers wound their way through the room offering the guests champagne and hors d'oeuvres from shining silver platters ringed with pink orchids.

Alison followed her grandmother to the front of the long receiving line.

"Oh, Mrs. Diamond!" Deirdre squealed. "We're so happy you've come to celebrate our special day!"

Alison tried not to gag as she looked over at Zoey. What a suck-up! Her grandmother would never tolerate such brownnosing. . . .

"Congratulations, dear. I'm pleased to be here," Tamara said with a small smile, stepping forward to give the district attorney an actual hug.

"Thank you for coming, Tamara," Zoey's dad said. "You look stunning, as usual."

"Thank you," Tamara said graciously, resting her hand on his arm. "Interesting event, Dante," she added as she straightened. "But very splendid. I would expect nothing less, of course."

Alison's ears burned. What was her grandmother up to? *Nobody is nice for no reason.* Tamara had actually been civil to Deirdre. And friendly toward the groom.

He must be more than an acquaintance, Alison thought. She hadn't seen the DA's name on any of the papers she stole, but she had a funny feeling as she watched the two of them together.

Alison fingered the beautiful pendant that sparkled on her neck. Her throat constricted. She had been so pleased when her grandmother had bought it for her. And the dress, too. But now she felt like a fool. She'd allowed herself to be bought.

Suddenly Alison felt as though the room were closing in on her. She couldn't breathe. *I've got to get out of here*, she thought.

She felt a tug on her arm and turned to see Zoey right behind her. "You okay?" Zoey said.

"I'm not feeling well," Alison whispered hoarsely, apologizing with her eyes. "I've gotta take off."

Zoey started to protest, then stopped when she saw the expression on her friend's face. "Okay. I'll call you later."

Alison smiled at Zoey, grateful for a real friend. Where would she be without her? Then she turned and saw that her grandmother was already surrounded by an admiring throng.

"Grandmother, I have a terrible headache," Alison lied after elbowing her way to her grandmother's side. "Would it be all right if I had Fernando take me home?"

Tamara acted as if she barely heard her. She was in her element now. "Of course, dear," she said with a wave of her well-jeweled arm. "Just send him back for me."

Alison nodded. Fifteen minutes later, she was heading up the grand staircase to her room.

Alison pushed the door open and stared, mouth agape. Her room was a mess. Someone had ransacked it. Every drawer had been pulled out and dumped. The contents of her closet were spilled all over the floor. Even her bed had been stripped, the mattress half on and half off the frame.

The bathroom was just as bad. Her makeup and accessories were spilled everywhere, and her favorite perfume bottle lay smashed on the tile floor.

Alison's hands clenched into fists as she stared at the mess — at the invasion — before her. This was too much. This crossed the line. Her grandmother must have had Alison's room ransacked, to look for the documents . . . or more likely as a warning. This was Tamara's way of letting Alison know what could happen if she ever decided to do anything with them. It was a not-so-subtle reminder that Grandmother Diamond was in complete control — and that Alison couldn't afford to have her as an enemy.

Her father's warnings echoed in Alison's head. Surely it was Tamara he'd been trying to caution her about. She wished she could talk to him now. She needed him more than ever. If she could just track him down . . . If he would just return her calls . . .

Alison bit her lip. She wouldn't cry. And she wouldn't be bullied. She would simply get out of there, leaving her grandmother with an empty room. As of right this minute, she no longer lived at the Diamond estate.

Chapter 33

Tom watched with disgust as his father and his new step-mom cut the cake.

"Come on, D5," Tom rooted quietly to himself as Deirdre held a large, frosted bite aloft. "Make him choke on it."

"That would be amusing," a voice behind him said. "But not very nice."

Tom whirled around and found himself face-to-face with X. What was she doing here? He hardly recognized her out of uniform. She looked amazing in a satin-and-lace camisole and an asymmetrical skirt.

"Nice to see you without your entourage," she said, leaning forward and straightening his tie as if she did it every day.

Tom felt his face redden. She was beautiful . . . and infinitely mysterious.

Getting lost in her dark eyes, Tom suddenly realized that he hadn't replied. "You mean my friends?" he stammered.

X chuckled. "Is that what you call them?" she said lightly. "I don't think I'd go that far."

"Tom," his father called abruptly. "We need you for photos." Ignoring X completely, DA Ramirez grabbed his son's arm and pulled him away.

"Dad, I was having a conversation!" Tom objected.

"I need you," DA Ramirez growled. "Come give your new stepmother a kiss for the camera. Right now."

That was the last straw. Tom's heart thudded in his chest. He couldn't keep his anger and suspicions in any longer. "Or what?" he demanded. "Or you'll drive me into the lake?"

DA Ramirez stared at his son, his face suddenly pale. But that fake smile never left his face. "You'd better watch yourself, kid," he snarled. "That water is deeper than you think." Then he rumpled his son's hair and laughed a little too loudly.

All at once the room shifted. Tom swallowed hard and steadied himself. His dad didn't even deny killing his mom!

"Come with me," DA Ramirez said, taking Tom by the arm again. But Tom was done.

"No," he said simply. "Your little circus act will have to finish the show without me." He shook his father off his arm and strode in the other direction. Within ten seconds Zoey was behind him.

"Are you all right?" she asked. "That looked intense."

"Get away from me," he snapped. "I'm sick of all of you."

Zoey recoiled. "I'm not them," she said quietly.

"Whatever," Tom replied, moving away from her. He needed to be alone. But as he pushed open the door he felt awful. He'd been chasing his best friend's girlfriend and treating his own twin like dirt. What was he turning into? At the end of it all, was he any better than his disgustingly slimy dad? *Yes*, he thought, *because I didn't kill anyone.*

Tom raced into the parking lot, pulling off his tie. His mind was whirling with what had just happened. He had no idea what he was going to do, he just had to move. As he made his way among the guests' Beamers and Jags and Mercedes, he spotted something familiar: the silver Audi TT.

Before he knew what he was doing, Tom ran toward the car. He yanked open the door . . . and stared, stunned. "It's *you*," he finally choked out.

Chapter 34

Alison watched the cabbie lift the last of her suitcases into the trunk and slam it closed before getting behind the wheel. As she settled into the leather seat and watched her grandmother's house grow smaller in the distance, she felt freer than she had in weeks. She was making the right decision. Living with her mostly incapable-of-getting-it-together father would be better than being Tamara's prisoner . . . or pet.

Suddenly an image from her childhood flashed in Alison's mind — her father comforting her after a bad fall from the jungle gym in the backyard. She'd scraped her knee in the dirt, and he'd scooped her up before she'd even had a chance to cry out.

"Super Daddy to the rescue!" he'd shouted, flying her into the house for some first-aid ointment and a bandage.

Alison smiled at the memory. Maybe together she and her father could be "super" again. It was definitely her best shot.

As screwed up as her family had been, she wanted to reconstruct it again. It was the best thing for all of them.

After what seemed like forever, the cab pulled up in

front of her house. Alison could tell right away that her father hadn't been keeping up with things. The garbage cans were still on the sidewalk outside the gate from the last pickup almost a week ago. The driveway was littered with newspapers. Her dad wasn't home, either — the house was dark.

Getting out of the cab, Alison looked up at her house. She felt exhilarated. Free from Tamara. Ready to help her mother fight — to fight for herself.

The cabbie set her bags next to the tall white pillars on the front porch. "Looks like nobody's home," he said. "You gonna be all right here all by yourself?"

Alison handed him a twenty. "Of course," she said. "My dad will be home any minute. He's expecting me," she added for good measure.

Nodding, the man got into his cab and drove away. When the wrought-iron gate had closed behind him, Alison unlocked the door and stepped inside. "Hello?" she called, not sure why. Her voice sounded echoey in the high-ceilinged home.

Alison reached for the light switch, flipped it on, and gasped. Her arms fell to her side and her bag slipped to the floor, landing with a thud.

Her house was empty. Literally. The furniture, the paintings, the books . . . all gone. *Everything* was gone.

Alison's footsteps were too loud as she ran from room to room searching for something — anything — from her old life.

"Daddy?" she called. A horrible loneliness flooded over her. Where was he?

And then she found it, in the built-in desk in her father's study. It was a plain white envelope with one word, in her father's handwriting, written on the outside: *Alison.*

Barely able to breathe, Alison ripped open the envelope and pulled out a folded piece of paper. As she opened it a smallish silver key fell to the floor. Her hands shaking, Alison looked down at the paper, hoping for an explanation.

The paper was blank.

Let your heart lead you...

In this follow-your-own-destiny romance series, your fate is in your hands. Choose carefully! You could end up broken-hearted... or you could land the boy of your dreams!

More Series You'll Fall in Love With

Heartland™
by Lauren Brooke

Nestled in the foothills of Virginia, there's a place where horses come when they're hurt. Amy, Ty, and everyone at Heartland work together to heal the horses—and form lasting bonds that will touch your heart.

www.scholastic.com/heartland

The AMAZING DAYS of ABBY HAYES®
by Anne Mazer

In a family of superstars, it's hard to stand out. But Abby is about to surprise her friends, her family, and most of all, herself!

www.scholastic.com/abbyhayes

DEAR DUMB DIARY
by Jim Benton

In Jamie Kelly's hilarious, candid (and sometimes not-so-nice) diaries, she promises everything she writes is true...or at least as true as it needs to be.

www.scholastic.com/deardumbdiary

Available Wherever Books Are Sold.

SCHOLASTIC and associated logos are trademarks and/or registered trademarks of Scholastic Inc.

■ SCHOLASTIC

FILLGIRL2

DUMPED AFTER FIVE YEARS, KATIE'S GOING ON TWELVE DATES IN SIX WEEKS.

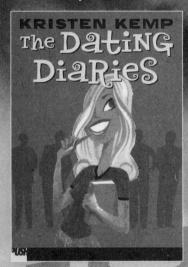

KRISTEN KEMP
The DATING DIARIES

I WILL SURVIVE

KRISTEN KEMP

love
sex
friendship
betrayal
depression
revenge!

love friendship sex betrayal depression revenge!

Katie James has been dating Paul since the seventh grade. Then, as the prom approaches, he dumps her. The last time she was on her own, she was wearing a training bra. Now she's about to see what she's been missing — and what it's like to date. But nothing quite goes the way she plans. Dating can be both frightful and fun — and Katie must learn how to be herself without a guy.

Ellen's boyfriend is cheating on her... with her best friend. Her sister is bratty. Her mom is having an affair with one of Ellen's most hateful teachers. And her second best friend is ruining their relationship by falling in love with her.

At first Ellen just wants to climb into bed and never get out again. But she comes up with a better idea: revenge. She's getting off and getting even—and she's going to find out how sweet (and sour) revenge can be.

www.this is*PUSH*.com

PUSH

KKDDIWS